MISPLACED
MEMORY

Michelle Gallo

To Rick, Anthony, Ricky, Natalie and Owen
Thank you for believing in me,
helping my dreams come true
and showing me the true meaning of love.

CHAPTER 1

Present

"Hannah! Hannah!"

  I can hear her cries in the distance.

"Hannah, this isn't funny. Come on, please. Please."

The voice is pleading with me to come out of hiding. I can hear her still calling, but it is becoming less and less clear, almost a distant whisper. The voice is so familiar, I can just place it.

It's Rebecca!

I can't tell where she is calling me from. I turn my head from side to side to see if I can hear better from one direction or the other.

Is she above me?

Her voice is growing muffled, starting to fade so that I can barely hear her anymore.

In the faint distance, a final time, "Hannah, let's go."

It's incredibly dark where I am. The type of pitch black when there are no stars in a cold winter night sky. It's warm out though almost mid May. This time of year, most nights don't go below 60 degrees, and the sky is usually lit up like the fourth of July.

How can it be this dark?

Frightened as a child without a nightlight to guide the way. My eyes are open, but there is nothing. I stop moving my head long enough to notice how quiet it is. There are no noises around me.I have never encountered such silence. There Should be frogs bellowing in the background, crickets chirping at the very least or even leaves rustling from above. Rebecca's voice has completely vanished. Deafening silence. I take a deep breath in. The air smells musky. Reminds me of my grandmother's old perfume. When she reaches in for a hug, I always move my face up, with my nose in the air. I almost hold my breath, because it's too strong to bear the whole smell in my nostrils at once. For only a moment sends the feeling of relief and calm through my body. Making me transcend from my current situation.

I wonder to myself, *is this real?* The darkness is impossible for me to ignore. I move my eyebrows up, widening my eyes to make sure they are open. I go to pinch myself, but I can't.

Where am I?

How the hell did I get here?

I start to feel the area around me, but my arms are stuck to my side. I am being held in this straight-arm, straight-legged position, but not with force from my surroundings. I don't have enough room to bend my elbows to feel what's stopping my arms from moving.

Is that a wall *on either side of me?*

I am stuck in a tight space. I start to panic. In these moments, usually I can count back from ten and calm myself into an even breathing pattern to relax. I can't seem to think of the words "ten, nine, eight" to even start the process. I bring my arms onto my waist, overlapping my hips, and bend my elbows over my stomach allowing my hands to my chest. Extending my fingers to my face, not without hitting the surface above me. Touching my hands to my rounded out face, I feel the moisture from my sweat, like morning dew drops on a rose bud, except warm. I reach in front of me, still not able to see anything. Wondering if I just lost my sense of sight, touching my fingertips to my eyes inevitably poking my pupal and knowing positively—without doubt—my eyes are open.

I can only bend my elbows about ten degrees; the hard surface is inches from my face. I spread my hands in front of me on the flat, smooth surface. Moving my hands slightly down only as far as chest level, my finger tip brushes over a knothole.

This surface is wood.

Guessing it's plywood similar to the wood we use to build the sets for Drama Club. My breathing grows heavier, and my chest feels like it is going to explode. My ears are pounding from how hard my blood is pumping through my veins. The deafening silence is broken by the blood pumping through my body, like white noise on a television.

I start to kick my feet downward, but I'm unable to bend my knees. Clenching my hands into fists, I pound them on the surface above. Screaming out in hopes that Rebecca is still close enough to hear me from outside of the prison I am in. As I'm kicking and pounding, there is dirt falling onto my body from above. The dirt is sticking to the sweat on my face. My hands and feet feel gritty, and it's only then I realize there is a sticky substance covering them. The smell of sodden earth mixes with a metallic smell that has interrupted the air, bile creeping into my throat. That's the moment it hits.

I am encapsulated in a wooden box buried in the ground.

But not dead. Yet.

How could this happen to me?

Why am I here?

The panic has completely taken over my body, the sweat from my forehead dripping into my eyes, along with my mascara. My eyes burn. My hands and feet are covered in what I can only believe is blood, the heavy smell of iron that has entered the air now taking over the musk. The blood dripping down my forearms and onto my clothes reminds me of a hot summer's rain. Likely self-inflicted from beating against the wooden surface that surrounds me.

I am dressed in my silk set of pajamas—shorts and a tank—and no shoes, as if I have just laid down to bed before I got here. Nothing is covering the rest of my body, like I was picked up from my bed and plopped into this box. My body is starting to go numb; I can't feel my hands or feet, undecided if it's from the pain that I have caused myself or from anxiety. Words are no longer forming on my lips to scream out.

If Rebecca was near before now, she would have heard me. She would have called from above and reassured me she was there. The shock of my reality has set in.

I am not getting out of this space.

My breathing has become labored. I am running out of time. Before long, there won't be enough air in these close quarters for me to breathe.

Does anyone know I am even here?

What am I going to do?

I forcefully shut my eyes, tears gushing down my cheeks. The blood, accompanied by the mascara from the night before, in a mixture floods my eyes. The burning sensation is so intense, like hot pokers have been seared through my eyelids and are penetrating my pupils.

Deep breath in, regaining minimal courage I may have left.

Ten, nine, eight, seven—Okay, that's good, Hannah. Seven is good. Let's try to make it to five.

Breathing deeply and heavily with each number I count. I have to pull together my sanity, but what in this moment is sane? Placing my hands to my face once more, I squeeze my rounded cheeks and jaw with my blood-soaked hands, trying to focus on counting back-wards so I can figure out what to do next.

KABOOM!

A loud earth-shaking noise comes from above, rattling the wooden box around me. My whole body tremors, like a small bomb has gone off directly next to me. I can only hope it isn't a bomb; this box wouldn't withstand one.

Are those footsteps above me?

Rebecca?

Have you found me?

Have you come back to free me?

KABOOM!

With another earth-shaking movement from above, this time my entire body goes into a convulsion, like I am having a seizure.

And just then, my mom's voice...

"Hannah!"

"Hannah! Can you hear me"?

"Wake up, Hannah. It's almost time to go"

My eyes jolt open as wide as they can be. Staring back at me is my mother's big brown eyes with just a small fleck of green in one. Her hands on my shoulders shaking me violently, I have a hard time focusing. All I see is her fluffy white robe in my face covering her light pajamas below.

I am at home in my bed, and she has woken me from my awful nightmare. I sigh with incredible relief.

I glance down quickly to see I am still in my blue silk pajamas with little orange carnations for design, and turn back to glimpse my mother's face. Still wide-eyed and taking in her image, her hair falls so perfectly, no matter what time of day. Annoying to me at the moment, I didn't get a single one of her features.Born out of place to the family and treated as such. Long, brown waves with just a hint of silver throughout, looking as though she has just freshly curled them. Pointed jawline; smile lines around her mouth. Barbie pink-colored bold lips, perky cheek bones that rest just below her eyes giving her a soft look. Manicured eyebrows, thin and every hair in its place. Round large brown eyes, sun-kissed tan on her smooth unblemished skin—unlike my own. Right now, a small wrinkle in her forehead from the concern. The worry on her face is palpable.

What would have happened if she didn't wake me?

Why did it take so much effort to distance myself from that hellish place?

"Mom, I'm okay," I say. "I must have been in a deep sleep and couldn't hear you."

"Clearly." The concern has left her face, and she has returned to the same look of subtle disapproval I am used to.

Sternly, she continues. "Get yourself up and ready. We are going to be late. We leave in 30. No later, and I mean it."

My room is simple, but perfect for everything I need. My bed lies in the middle of the room. On the left side is a white canopy, upholstered metal that has storage space underneath. The headboard and footboard are white tufted, soft material. Sheer white curtains draped from the top to add a touch of elegance to my otherwise disaster that surrounds the bed. My sheets are off-white, with more pillows than any one person needs. My walls are a plain, very light gray lined with posters of the music I have been listening to recently, as well as Broadway musicals. I just recently added a poster of Wicked to my collection on the wall. The music has been at the top of my playlist for about a month now. I don't have a ton on my wall but a few favorites: Les Miserable, Mama Mia,and Phantom of the Opera, of course the good classics. The music posters, only a few rock artists mostly 80's hair band stuff, nothing really new school. Weird mix I'm sure to anyone that walks in here. Not that anyone comes to visit my room. A cork board above my dresser is lined with favorite photography shots that I have taken. A wooden dresser handed down from who knows how many relatives sits directly across from my bed. Decorated with perfumes, my moms added touch to my room. There is a jewelry box that is always open, along with an assortment of skin care items my mom picks up on her travels.

My room overlooks the front of our yard with a beautiful three-pane picture window. My curtains are also white and always drawn open. No matter how many times I pick up my clothes, my floor continuously serves as a laundry basket. I take my clothes off, throw them on the floor and they sit until I decide I am ready to do something with them. I have papers from school and open books intermingled with my clothes on the floor. I tend to live in what I consider organized chaos. The unorganized mess eases my mind for reasons unknown.

On either side of my window, wrapping around the bottom, I have a bookshelf built into the wall. It's my favorite part of this room. It's like having my own personal library right here beside me. I have books on the right that have never been read and on the left that I have read countless times. One of my re-reads is the book IT by Stephan King. Seeing the book is intimidating by the sheer size but the story is amazing. One of my most read and most owned authors by far.

Staring around my room, I couldn't be any happier than to have woken up here. My safe space.

"Are you even listening?" My attention is drawn back to my mom, away from all the things that give me comfort.

She shuffles from the bed, heading for the doorway, turns around to look at me once more. Taking me in only for a moment like I'm a little girl with a cut on my knee and she can cure it with a hug and some helpful words. Her lips part ever so slightly—she wants to ask me more. Inquiring now would lead to a conversation she doesn't really have time for. The moment passes as quickly as it came on, instead of asking anything further.

She simply says, "Are you sure you're alright? You're white as a ghost."

I contemplate telling her the horror that was my dream to see if she really wants to listen as I elaborate on the subject.

I decide to just go with the usual response.

"I had a bad dream. I'm fine. I'll be down in ten."

She nods and turns leaving the doorway, away to her room just across the hall.

Was that actually just a dream?

I rise from my bed, and stroll into my bathroom. My bathroom—which most would consider a luxury—is attached to my bedroom, so I don't have to move very far. My mom decorated it when we moved in a few years ago. I have a large sink and vanity area for my makeup and everyday use items. Dark wooden cabinets are decorated with some fake wood pattern, when I rub my hands across it feels like laminate. Above my sink is a round mirror lined with an aluminum frame, dark in color to match the cabinets. My bathroom mats are black plush, so soft on my feet in the morning. The shower has a rainforest-style head that trickles from above while I'm in it. The glass doors that surround it have a film for privacy, so the tile is distorted from the outside.

Looking in the mirror, I begin to examine my face, hands and feet. I assume my mother may have shown more apprehension if I was covered in blood and my mascara had run down my face with dried tears. I am surprised to look in the mirror and see my face completely clean, instead of covered in blood and soil. My hands and feet are no longer sticky or banged up, no open wounds. I grab a brush, trying to tame my red curly mane. My hair is soft to the touch, but appears coarse. Tight ringlet curls that intertwine with one another. Brushing through, I pull it up to a formable ponytail. Take a good look at my green eyes, making sure I don't look like I have been crying all night. Wiping the corners of my eyes to get the crust that formed overnight.

Not a freckle out of place; everything is in order.

I grab a towel from the shelving unit above my toilet—the only thing neat in my entire room because my mom stocks it. Run the hot water until it's too hot to touch and then turn on cold so it's bearable for my face. Wash up, slap on some new mascara and go away to the dresser for some clothes.

As I open up the drawer of my wooden dresser, I shudder. Chills run down my entire body, and goosebumps form on my arms. That smell... That earthy, musty smell brings back the entire dream like I am planted right back into the ground in a box. Grabbing my slim, distressed jeans, I slam the drawer in disgust. I begin breathing heavily. I'm forcing myself into panic. Telling myself to calm down, I think, It *was just a dream. You were never in a box.*

Ten, Nine, Eight, Seven, Six, Five... Deep breath.

Get it together, Hannah. It didn't happen.

Snatching up a black v-neck shirt from the floor, I gave it a smell check, realizing it probably should have been ironed before wearing it. Throwing it over my head anyways, I look down at the wrinkles that have stretched mostly out over my chest. *Eh, this seems fine.* I nod to myself in approval, grab my black backpack with my lucky blue rabbit's foot and fly down the stairs.

My mom—per usual—didn't beat me down here. I snag an apple from the porcelain white dish in the middle of the kitchen table. Pull a few random papers from my backpack, and I set up shop on the kitchen island, looking over the homework I should have completed throughout the weekend.

The weekend seems to have escaped me. Saturday night was the party and bonfire and now it's Monday. How did i not complete my assignments yesterday, why does it seem like Sunday didn't exist.

I went to look for Rebecca in the woods and woke up to my mom shaking me.

Where was Rebecca?

Did I find her?

What did I drink?

Maybe I ate something that didn't agree with me.

Before I can overthink the premise of my thought, my mom comes shuffling down the carpeted stairs, managing not to touch the white railing to the right of her on the way down. In a perfectly pressed black pants-suit and button-down pink shirt below her blazer. Looking immaculate, hair completely untouched by getting dressed or roaming about her room still in perfect form, a leather briefcase in hand. Always coming down the stairs like she is falling, looking like she has forgotten something. She glides through the living room and into the kitchen, standing at the table and staring at the bowl that is missing only an apple.

"That's all you're going to eat?" she says. With my back turned to her, knowing she has her hands up in the air, and she's giving an eye roll in disapproval. Pretty standard when she accepts my unpleasant answer.

"Yes." A simple reply that makes her wrinkle her nose.

I turn towards her, and with a sigh, she replies, "Alright. The doctor is waiting for us."

Our relationship wasn't always like this. My mom and I were really close as I was growing up. We used to do everything together—shopping, nails, talking about boys, talking about my dreams, college, what's next in my life, how work was going for her. Every night for as long as I can remember, she would go into the freezer, grab whatever ice cream we had, separate towering scoops into two bowls, top hers with chocolate curls, and bring them over to the couch. We would watch TV—nothing important, just whatever was on—and enjoy each other's company. I could blame our growing apart on being a junior in high school, or hormones and body changes forcing me to outgrow the need to be so close to her. The divorce had a lot to do with it too.

Since she and my dad were constantly fighting, it was almost like she resented me for wanting to see him. The divorce is an event we don't ever talk about, even though someday, I would like to understand what happened there. Since my dad moved, we see each other less frequently than I would like, but it's not a situation I can help. We don't talk often. He doesn't have much access to the phone, but when he does call, my mom acts like it's a terrible inconvenience for me to have a conversation with him.

Her and I don't engage in unwarranted conversation much anymore, especially about dad. He is completely and utterly off-limits in this house. We have tried in the past, but it always becomes "I'm dramatic", or "too opinionated", or the worst—"just like my father". Our conversations are so few, we barely know each other anymore. I have not even an inkling what she is doing at work. She used to talk about what she could do about her cases frequently, sometimes even asking my opinion or how I felt about a situation. She definitely has no idea what I have been up to. Monday nights are generally the only ones we have any at length conversations, and even those are short, sweet and vague. Resorting to silence or minimal communication suits us just fine.

"Let's get going if you won't eat anything more." She knows that I won't, but has to slide that little jab in.

We are not rich, but I have never heard my mom utter a peep of struggling or not being able to afford something. It helps, I'm sure, that I am involved in very little that requires funds to be readily available like sports, clubs, or trips. We live in a nice suburban neighborhood just on the outside of the town. On weekends, kids line the sidewalks and the road playing toss, dodgeball and capture the flag, few parents out watching, all tending to their own outdoor activities. Each child scurries to the doors of their modern homes when the street lights come on. Five or so homes on each side of the street leading to the cul-de-sac at the end. Enough yard on the front of each to have a plentiful garden and bushes to divide each home from the next. Some houses have a two-car garage. Ours happens to be one of the houses with only a one-car. The garage door opens in front of us as I climb into my mom's newer silver Cadillac Escalade. Such a big car for just the two of us.

In the car, driving to the appointment, we barely speak a word to each other. The noise of the radio in the background from whatever country station she listens to is enough to cure the silence between us. Neither of us feels obligated to speak.

This particular drive is a weekly ritual. I usually take the bus to school, but since the divorce, which was quite a while ago, I am forced to see a psychiatrist. There was a lot of terrible banter and accusations between my parents, and the good doctor is supposed to help me navigate.

Her name is ironically Dr. Psych.

CHAPTER 2

Present

Walking into Dr. Psych's office makes me anxious. However, she may be the only person other than Rebecca who even knows the real me. I can be transparent, which is a comforting thought.

The office is set up like a house with a set of white French doors upon entry. The walls are a beige color, it feels like a warm hug. There are a few brown metal waiting chairs with plain cushions, which no one is ever sitting in this early. The carpet is a standard mix of browns, like the ones on the showroom floor at the home improvement stores. The one that every busy mom has in their house to hide all the stains. The entryway is more luxurious with a dark Italian style tile. Makes me wonder how it is always so clean here. It's not like we take off our shoes. A large oak desk that sits in the middle of the waiting area where you check in and the receptionist bubbly as ever on a Monday morning jumps from her chair. I never remember her name, but she seems to remember every detail about me.

"Hi Han. Hi Trish." The receptionist greets us as we walk past the beautiful stained glass windows towards her desk. For some reason it bothers me when people call my mom Trish. Especially when someone should be a professional and greets her like they are best friends. I feel like Trish is so personal, even though everyone calls her that instead of Patricia.

She's just able to look over the top of the desk standing up. She is shorter than most freshmen I know. For working in a doctor's office, she is very homely in her appearance—not casually dressed, but not quite dressed up. Flat black shoes that her black pants pretty much cover; I'm surprised she doesn't trip on them as she walks. A dress top, but unlike my mom's pantsuit she wears just a simple button-down with a collar. Her mousy brown hair tied back with a pencil sticking out like a librarian. I'm not sure why she feels comfortable enough to call me Han, but politely, I nod, and my mom trots right to the desk to share her weekly news. You would think they were old time friends sharing the gossip of the day. I head towards the brown chairs, and not even a minute later, Dr. Psych is standing at the door behind the larger-than-necessary reception desk.

Dr Psych is much taller than the receptionist. I look up to her, and I am 5' 6". She wears a neatly pressed black pencil skirt with a button-down top of some plain rose color that matches. Over her dress clothes, she always has on a white lab coat, a few pencils in one pocket and her hand in the other. With a large smile, she looks at my mom and then at me, and says "good morning" to us as individuals. This must be a doctoral technique to make us feel good, which I think might work. Her hair is in a well-manicured brunette bun, not a single hair out of place. Her eyes are brown, but sparkle with her smile. She doesn't seem to have a single wrinkle on her face. I am envious of her smile—straight, white teeth that shine so bright they are blinding to look at, behind her nude lipstick so her lips don't stand out past her teeth.

The hand out of her pocket motions my entrance to her office.

"Are you ready for the day, Hannah?" As if I have any choice in the matter.

Her tone of voice is so calm and collected it makes me feel like her life must be so put together outside of this place. I don't know how she can remain so tranquil dealing with crazies all day. I imagine her with her cat, Bruno, sitting down next to a fireplace, sipping on some aged wine and reading a quiet book with a blanket over the both of them. I don't think she is married; I have never noticed a ring or a picture of a husband. Plenty of pictures of Bruno who is an 18-pound tabby cat, though, and he's pretty cute.

I haven't sat down yet, so I shuffle around the desk and into her office. She waves her hand again to motion me to my favorite chair—a gray indoor swing chair. I take a giant leap into the chair, and she closes the door behind her. Sitting quietly and swaying on the chair, not looking her directly in the eye, wondering if she already somehow knows about this dream. As if she was perhaps a fly on my wall in my room, watching me sleep. Managing to give myself the creeps, goosebumps down my arms, I shake it off and look up to see her staring at me. I shrink in my seat. Maybe she hears thoughts too?

"Did you bring your journal today?"

I dig through my backpack, not knowing which pocket I left it in, papers falling all over from unfinished work that I just shoved in here. Some random screws that I have zero idea how they ended up in my backpack. I don't have the time to ponder their presence in my bag at the moment. Dr. Psych will think I am stalling intentionally if I take too long to retrieve my journal from my bag, which I have admittedly done before. I am not in a place today to hear her condescending tone towards me. I don't even know what most of the stuff in here is for, but I find my journal, and pull out a suede skin color notebook with a labyrinth pattern on the front cover.

When I first started to see Dr. Psych, she bought me one just like this. Since then, I have filled two with my daily thoughts and nonsense. The idea is to use it daily to record my thoughts and feelings. It helps me to release. Plus, it helps give Dr. Psych insight to my frame of mind and where my thoughts live. The labyrinth on the front is basically a maze, but the meaning behind it is spiritual transformation. I hand her the notebook; she opens the latest entry which was more than a week ago.

She never reads it aloud, only to herself.

"Today is Monday, isn't it Hannah?'

"Yes." I'm puzzled by her questioning what day today is as I see her every Monday.

"Why is the last entry from over a week ago? You left my office on Monday last week and we discussed the importance of this at length. You haven't written a single entry since that conversation."

I scramble my brain to think of a witty response, but know that never goes over well in this office. Instead, I'm really trying to recall why I haven't written in the book since last week. I pulled it out Friday—why didn't I write that day? Recalling the day and the events, I think, *Oh that's right! I was at the mall, and Rebecca showed up.*

What have I been doing that has me so distracted? Why can't I remember what has been going on the last few days? The chalkboard of my mind has been wiped clean, no memory or even a trace of what I have been up to.

"Honestly I don't know why it's blank."

She seems to accept my answer. "Okay. Have you been taking your medicine daily?"

Thinking about that before I reply, I really haven't no real reason to lie. She's going to know. She's psychic. "No, I don't think I have."

"Well, that would explain not writing in your journal. Tell me—Have you been experiencing any other issues? Hallucinations, missing blocks of time, rage, scattered thoughts?"

"Yes, no rage that I have been aware of, though. There was a dream that I had last night that I can't imagine where I even thought of such a wild idea." I go on to explain the dream in details that I can recall.

Dr. Psych cracks the code. This explains the dream, the missing time from the weekend before and feeling of absolute loss. I have been pretty scattered as of late. Now that I know what's going on with me, I feel my shoulders drop, almost at ease with myself and at peace that I am not completely losing it.

"Hannah, you really need to take your medicine on a regular basis. You know the side effects of not taking it timely, and what issues you may have. With you and your dad's diagnosis, it's very important, especially with a visit from him coming up this week. As for the notebook, we discussed this last week, so I won't focus on that hard again this week, but for progress it is important we keep track of where your head is at. Are we on the same page here?"

She isn't yelling but I know she is serious. Scolding me for not following my instructions, I do know the consequences for not. When we first started seeing each other, all those years ago, she made it clear that this only works if I put in the work. It is constant effort on my part, but we have made progress.

She presses the fold in her skirt down and pushes her glasses back to her perfectly maintained eyebrows. I nod in acceptance that I haven't been doing the right things for myself and my improvement, and continue on with my swinging.

"Now that we have gotten that out of the way, let's talk about this dream you had and put some meaning behind it. Shall we?"

I describe in great detail my dream to her—from Rebecca calling out to me all the way to how I was woken up by my mom but thought I was still in a wooden casket on the ground.

"Tell me... Who is Rebecca? Is she a new friend from school or someone you just started seeing in the last week?"

I pause for a moment in disbelief that we have never spoken about Rebecca in this room. Rebecca and I have been inseparable for months. Spending every Friday together at the mall shopping for the newest outfits, hanging out on the weekends during parties. Even if I leave out sneaking out to the parties, I still should have mentioned her at some point. Rebecca and I bonded over a book in the library ,and ended up in drama club together later. She played the lead role in the school musical.

"Rebecca was at the library one afternoon while I was searching in the non-fiction section for a book to do some research. She was looking for the same book. We have the same history teacher, different periods of the day. I told her that I would check the book out at a different time and she said that was nonsense, we could work on it together in the library. We studied for hours that day trying to write papers that didn't match, so the teacher wouldn't call us out for working together on an individual study piece. I consider her my friend. After a few months of hanging out together, the drama club started. She scored the role for Belle in the school musical, and I was on stage crew."

"Aw, and how does that make you feel that she was in the musical and you were on the crew?" The tone of concern in her voice for my feelings is very apparent. As if not having a role in the musical would ruin me.

I hate it when she uses doctor phrases. It's not often, but she does do it.

"I was happy for her; I adore Rebecca. She is amazingly talented. She's the captain of the cheer squad and dating the top basketball player. She's a beautiful tall blonde with a perfect figure, with excellent makeup that makes her face glow in the sun. Everyone is positive Rebecca and Nate will be prom king and queen this year. They are just perfect together. She's really just so pretty, funny and overall, just a good person. And for her to be friends with me just tops the cake for how great she is."

"Okay, Hannah, I'm glad you have found a friend. It sounds like you have a lot of admiration for this Rebecca. However, I am concerned how sudden this friendship is."

Suddenly? But she really doesn't know, so I can't fault her for assuming we just instantly became friends. That doesn't happen in high school.

"It's not sudden. I just haven't brought it up in this office."

"Is there a reason why?" Her eyebrows raise at me with questions.

"I guess I was nervous about how you would feel about me getting close to someone, or that you might tell my mom and she would start to watch my every move like a hawk again."

"That's a valid concern to have given your adventures a few months back. I can understand the concern, and I appreciate you being so honest and opening up about this relationship now."

"This isn't a relationship. We aren't together. I do admire her, but not in that way."

"No need to be on the defense. You can care, love and admire someone without being in a sexual relationship with them. We would call that platonic."

As soon as sexual comes from her lips, I shiver and goosebumps run down my arms. What a terrible word to use here, makes me feel just gross.

"Let's dive into this friendship more next week. Please write about it in your journal and tell me some more about your adventures." She pauses. "Let's chat about this dream, shall we?"

Again, as if the choice is available for me to say no. "Of course."

"Great, so tell me—Have you always had a fear of being buried alive, or do you think this has a deeper meaning than just being stuck in a box in the ground?" She wants me to lead the conversation, so I suppose that's what I'll do.

"Actually, I don't think I have a fear of death at all. I think that I am projecting my fear of being alone."

"Very insightful, Hannah. Impressive, even. So why do you fear being alone?"

"Doesn't everyone, Doctor? I can't be the only patient you see that fears being alone." I know this response will trigger Dr. Psych to deflect the situation living alone herself, which is where I want things to end.

"I suppose most do. With your visit with your dad this weekend, make sure your medicine is in check as of today. Is there anything we can do here to help ease that fear to maybe help with those dreams?"

"Well it's been pretty helpful to have Rebecca. It makes me feel like maybe I am not alone or at least won't always be."

"I think that's great. If there is something that I or maybe your mom can do to help, do keep us in the know. All we want is to help you progress, Hannah. Keep that in mind. See you next week?"

And just like that, I have escaped the need to dive deeper into this dream.

She poses it as a question instead of a statement, because she knows I will be here next week. I am a little taken aback that she was so focused on my friendship with Rebecca. She really thinks that this was a sudden movement, like those people that meet and get married within the first few months of knowing each other. Even though we discussed the dream, I know I can't escape the conversation coming back in the following weeks as easily as I have now. Maybe I'll write about it, and it will open up my mind to what is really happening.

Dr. Psych hands me my notebook looking down at me, her eyes telling me I better get my act together and write in this damn book. If I do, maybe I can alleviate these dreams and wild thoughts by getting them on paper and out of my head. I throw my notebook back into one of the pockets of my backpack and give a good shove downward so it's eaten up by the other contents.

Now that we know my meds are an issue, hopefully, we won't have any more of that to discuss. As we are getting ready to leave, Dr Psych takes my mom to the side and has a mini recap of our conversation, which is pretty normal protocol after our visit. I stand and chit chat with the receptionist for the last few minutes while they wrap up. My mother turns to me with that wrinkle in her forehead much like the one she had this morning.

Wheels in my head turning like a hamster running on a wheel trying to win a marathon. What could she have said to my mom? Did she just express her concern about my relationship or maybe even my admiration for Rebecca and divulge what she thinks is a secret intimacy? Did she just tell her everything about the dream? She wouldn't have done that.

Would she?

The feeling of panic is starting to come on. I stare at the ground, trying to refocus myself and slow my breathing. *Let's not make a big deal in case Dr Psych said nothing and you're overreacting*, I think.

"Goodbye Trish. Goodbye Han. Have a good day you lovely ladies," the receptionist says as we are closing the last inch of the French doors from behind us.

I am actually afraid to ask my mom what Dr Psych said to her. Usually, I don't even care to ask.

Why do I care now?

CHAPTER 3

Present

Wow this place looks like a zoo—camera vans are all over the bus loop wrapping around the side of the school as we are pulling in for my mom to drop me off. There has to be at least a hundred people standing in the front of the school building below the front steps, microphones in hand and cameras pointed at the front door, seemingly waiting for someone to come outside or give directions. Whispering amongst themselves as I exit the car, they rush over to me like a herd of goats waiting to be fed the next juicy detail to put in their weekly story. I turn back fast to see if my mom is still behind me. She's on the phone watching, shooing me to advance forward to the stairs. Turning back towards the school, the mob has now collected around me. I am engulfed like moths to a flame.

"What is your name?" the first reporter says, shoving the black foam piece of the microphone to my mouth. I turn my head to avoid the microphone, but directly in front of me is another.

"Did you go to school here?"

"Did you know her?"

Not replying to any of them, I put my head down into my hands, grasping my face, fingers spread just enough to see the ground below, trying to make my way towards the stairs. Bobbing and weaving my way through the people, I finally make it through the sea of microphones and cameras. I reach the first step and advance to the second. As I reach the first plateau with two ahead before the doors, I turn around. There they all stand, still shouting questions, but not one toe has stepped on the stairs behind me. I imagine an invisible line like a dog fence between us, one they're not able to cross.

The expression on my face tells a story that I am clueless as to why they are here or what they want from me.

"Did you know the missing girl?" the reporter shouts as I turn away to make my way up the cobblestone steps quicker than I did before.

Reaching the top of the final plateau, I feel safe at such a far distance from them. I turn my left foot to position myself, turning around to face them once more. They're mouthing the words "who is the missing girl" as I turn my head.

Principal Martinez is standing in front of me, grabs my shoulders and shuffles me into the open door. Shushing me as we walk quickly through the wooden doors, seconds later he's closing them from behind us, the fastest I have ever seen him move.

"Boy it sure is crazy out there. Did you answer any of the reporter's questions as you were walking in?"

Standing in front of me with a look of fright in his eyes, peering down at me not so patiently waiting for me to answer no. Giving me the chills, I shake my head to indicate that I hadn't. He shuffles me into the main office, signs a hall pass and sends me on my way.

Principal Martinez is a very well-kept man, short and round with a bald head, but always in his best dressed. His skin is lightly tanned. His suits are always a unique pattern—today, a paisley and gray striped with matching vest and light tan shirt under. He always has a pocket watch and chain hanging from his suit pocket. Like an elderly man, there's a chain hanging from around his neck, and affixed at either side of the chain is each side of his glasses. He doesn't wear them often, but always has them around his neck. His features are all dark, except his eyes are a caramel color—very majestic in the sunlight.

I take myself out of the gaze Principal Martinez has me in, and I think back.

I wonder if my mom is still outside of the school. I didn't see her drive off, and she didn't seem concerned with me getting to the door through the maze of people. Is she still sitting in her car, or talking to reporters, or did she just drive off to the firm without a second thought or glance?

I have escaped the clutches of Principal Martinez, who gladly wrote me a late pass after making sure that I absolutely did not speak to the press. Making my way to the second period, I have already missed first and the bell marking the beginning of second.

The thought lingers— *Who was the missing girl?*

Does everyone but me know who is missing? Does this have anything to do with Saturday night? Did someone get hurt after we left? Why was Principal Martinez so concerned about talking to the press? I wonder if my mom knows anything at the firm yet?

Drowning in my own thoughts, with my head down, rushing even though I am always late on Mondays and its expected, I realize I missed the door for my class, which probably looks super suspicious given the circus outside. I swiftly turn around and grab the door handle.

Entering my history class, half the cheerleaders are sitting in a circle whispering in low tones, trying not to wake the substitute teacher. No instruction is taking place, some boring cowboy movie animates, for the class to sit quietly and absorb the information. I grab the seat closest to the window in the back of the room. The group of girls stare at me as I walk past, not saying anything directly to me. The tones are so low that I can't make out any actual words they are saying to one another.

Are they talking about me? Is that why they are looking over here? It's the whole crowd that was at the bonfire on Saturday—Does this have to do with that? Why is so much missing in my thoughts? Could this really be just from my medicine?

I would consider myself an outcast for the most part. I keep to myself; I have no friends other than Rebecca. She and I only speak when she isn't busy, and we only hang out alone, just the two of us. She doesn't have history this period, she has it fourth, so I can't ask her what is going on. I have so many questions from Saturday night to this morning. When I see her, undoubtedly, Rebecca will have way more information. Does she know the missing girl?

I am the only teenager without a cell phone in this school, so I can't text her either. Mom has this rule that I should be focused on my studies and treatment without outside distractions that may cause what she calls "ripples" in my day. My mom is a defense attorney at a hoity-toity law firm in the city, so we don't watch the news in my house either. My only contact with the outside world is when Rebecca and I go places, or when I stay late to take pictures for the school yearbook. Joining the drama club gave me some extra socialization too, but that's over now that we completed the musical for the year.

The movie the teacher put on for the class isn't over, but the bell rings and everyone rushes to the door like goldfish trying to get a bite before the fish next to him, prepared to exchange gossip in the halls before third. I have chemistry for my third period. I saunter through the halls, barely making eye contact with anyone. My head is always down, hand touching my shoulder strap to my backpack for security to know it's still attached. I enjoy chemistry class, and the teacher Ms. Murphy. She is in a wheelchair, a much larger woman, comfortably dressed in a one-color dress that looks like a nightgown. Today it's maroon. Her hair like salt and pepper shakers exploded to make it wild and free. She's incredibly feisty, although I have never asked how she really ended up in the wheelchair. I doubt she would give me the correct answer. I think that might be insensitive. I imagine it isn't socially acceptable to just confront someone and ask "Why are you really in a wheelchair?" She does give plenty of reasons, but none the same as the last.

"Keep coming in late to class, you know how I got these wheels? I was late to class and my teacher snapped at me one too many times with a ruler."

"You know how I got these wheels? I mouthed off one too many times to my mom and she slammed my legs in a door."

"You know how I got these wheels? I mixed those chemicals you have in your hand and set my pants on fire."

Never sure if any of what she said was true or not, or if she was only trying to be funny.

Our studies as of late are compiled of chemicals and making our own solvents, which I suppose could be useful. I like the hands-on applications of this class instead of just sitting and reading from a book. We sit in our assigned seats. I am directly in the front of the classroom; we only sit for a few minutes to collect the day's details and then advance off to our benches for work. Every station has a burner, an array of glass beakers to use, red cotton cloths to keep our stations clean, and a paper—new everyday for that day's assignment to be completed for the lab.

Continuing our studies on solvents, our lab this week is what certain solvents do to solids or if they have any effect on them at all. For example, a piece of paper is put into water, ethanol and acetone. We do the experiment and record our results, then we can make a hypothesis about the next item to be dipped. I am using a pair of tongs to put a wooden children's block into the acetone, and I hear Murph yell as clearly as can be over the chatter of the other students, "Hold it there, boy!"

Everyone in the room freezes and turns to her making her way through the chairs on her electric scooter. I put the block down on the counter, and turned all the way around to face one of the other stations behind me.

There stands Ken—a tall awkward boy who has decided that he isn't going to put solids in the liquids, but instead mix the solvents to see what happens. In most cases, Ms. Murphy indulges in our interest and lets us experiment as long as it's safe. In this case, it isn't safe, and we had learned this particular mixture in class a few weeks ago.

Chlorine bleach with acetone... He was about to make chloroform.

"Kenny, you know damn well that's not okay. I can't have you lying on my floor for the next few hours. I'll have put you in the closet until you come-to. We don't need another missing student today. Come on now."

Clearly kidding that she would put anyone in a closet. She was actually pretty compassionate when anyone was ill or hurt. One time Tim sliced his finger open while we were cutting for an experiment. Her scooter went so fast, it knocked over two chairs in the process just to make sure he was alright. She even carries a medical kit right in the bottom of her electric scooter in the event anyone needs anything.

He knows she isn't kidding; he stops instantly, laughs it off and returns to the original assignment. Even Ms. Murphy knows who the missing girl is.

Am I close enough to her to ask? How could she joke about it so soon?

Shaking off the thought because I know that I am not her favorite student, I return to my block and acetone.

From this classroom, I can see the front of the building. There are windows all around the lab space, and more people have gathered with signs and cameras at the front of the school. There are at least four police cars with their lights on spinning around. Still, no one has slipped who is missing or what is going on outside. I haven't run into Rebecca in the halls yet to ask her what she thinks.

The announcement sound blares overhead, and everyone is awaiting the directions from the speaker.

"The following students please report to Principal Martinez's office..."

A list of names—all from the cheerleading squad and a few basketball players, including Nate—are announced. The speaker repeats itself annoyingly, and then turns off.

Ms. Murphy turns to us. "Must have been a pretty wild party this weekend, kids. Go on, report and come back when you're done. No rompas in the hallways, ya hear?"

A handful of students stand up and advance to the door.

"The rest of you, back to solvents."

Fourth period is finally here. Each class has dragged an extra hour than the last. We are almost through this day. What a relief that it's finally over.

Geometry is the last class I have. We had homework that I didn't even attempt to do, but I know the paper is in here somewhere. Digging through my bag for the third time today to retrieve my work. Curious, there is a red cloth like the ones from Chemistry in the bottom of my back pack. Along with screws that are still rolling around from this morning in Dr. Psych's office

Where did those come from?

Do we even have screws at my house?

Did I steal a rag from chemistry this morning?

Has this been in there all along?

More missing pieces...

Without trying to overthink, I stand up and walk to the back of the classroom, tossing the rag and the screws in the garbage. Looking up as I walk back to my seat, my eyes catch onto Nate's. He is staring me down, narrow brow and red eyes, but that might be from crying. Why has he been crying? Why does he have so much hatred for me?

I snagged my seat, and found the paper from the week before that we are about to go over and can't help but drift into my own state of mind.

I haven't seen Rebecca once today. Come to think of it, I haven't seen the squad members that were called to office since Chemistry started. The missing girl must be connected to Saturday. Is it possible they are all in trouble for underage drinking? Are they all suspects? Who even bought the alcohol that they were drinking? Do they have something to do with the missing girl? Is it one of them?

I raise my hand to excuse myself to the bathroom, grab a pass and run.

The door flies open. I run to a sink, grab both sides with my hands and squeeze. I look up to the round mirror and see my pudgy face with freckles staring back at me. Hair crazy like I just threw up. Counting to myself.

Ten, nine, eight, seven, six, five, deep breath.

This is my second panic attack today. Why do I do this to myself?

Hannah, get your shit together. No one is in trouble. Everything is okay. The missing girl is a random event, and we are all fine. Breathe.

I forget for a moment that I am in a school bathroom. There could be students in the several stalls that line the wall behind me. I turn the water on, throw some on my face and stare at myself for a minute. I use my wet hands to tame my hair, then dispense some paper to dry my face and hands. Toss the paper towel in the trash on my way out, and head to finish class so that I can get out of this school for the day.

It's been a weird day. First the dream, the talk with Dr. Psych, my mom acting strange afterwards, then the mystery of the missing student who remains nameless. Heading to the buses to go home, I don't see Nate or any of the cheer squad that had been taken to the office. Usually they are crowded in front of the buses, watching everyone leave while they wait for practice.Nate and Rebecca typically the center of attention holding one another in the middle of the team circle. I jump onto the bus steps, and go to find my seat, an empty window seat looking towards the school. Looking out the window to monitor the kids walking from the school towards their cars and buses to conclude the day. The police cars are still in place from the third period, and the camera vans as if they haven't been touched since this morning.

Just then, in the swarm that has now moved toward the bus line, out of the corner of my eye, I spot it.

I see a poster in a lady's hands. My eyes are wide and not blinking for what seems like an hour in disbelief.

I see who is on the poster. The missing girl.

This can't be real.

CHAPTER 4

Friday, Three Days Ago

It's the Friday before the girl went missing.

Rebecca and I have started a ritual of meeting at the mall on Friday nights to go shopping before the mall becomes a madhouse for the weekend. After all, the captain of the squad has to look her very best and be in the latest clothing when she makes her appearance at each of the events. Now that Rebecca and Nate have become an item, she is constantly worried about how she is going to look everywhere she goes. Rebecca has a flawless sense of style. If we voted for silly things like best dressed, she would be it to a T. I don't think she has ever worn the same combination of clothes twice. It seems like she has an endless supply of clothing in her house.

After seeing her house, that is also entirely possible.

Games are Saturday evenings; I have been doing the photography for the games since the beginning of this year when I forced myself to try the Yearbook Committee. I didn't realize then how involved I was going to be in every school-sanctioned event. I am responsible for all sporting events for all teams, from Mod A all the way to Varsity, as well as girls and boys. The shots are "before and after", as well as what they call "Lightning shots" in the game so I stay for the duration of each. The "money shots" are of the team in action—scoring goals, making a touchdown, an amazing kick. I take pictures throughout the whole game, and then edit on my laptop and give the best ones to the school newspaper publisher. I save some to choose, and those will be used in the final layout of the yearbook. As much as it sounds like so much work, the reality is, if I hadn't joined this, I wouldn't have known about the parties or gotten involved with Rebecca like I have been.

When the game has come to an end, everyone heads to their houses, grabs dinner with their families, and changes their clothes to prepare for the festivities of the evening. Some have their own vehicles, some walk to meet up with one another and hop a ride. Pending the spot to hang out, some can walk there. Other than drinking, nothing really goes on at the parties—lots of gossip, and right now, discussing who is going to prom with who and what dresses everyone is wearing.

Prom is right around the corner, and we have been spending so much effort preparing that I have lost track of time. As a part of the

Yearbook Committee, it is also my responsibility to help with ideas on food, theme and décor. I am definitely not good at any of this. I pretty much just listen and follow the lead of those in charge. We are going with Disney to stick with our school theme. Like our musical this year—Beauty and the Beast—it's been an ongoing thing. I don't have a date, but I will be there with a camera in hand for yearbook photos. This year, I was elected to be the photographer for each of the couples that come through. Apparently, I am good at capturing the best moments.

The main entrance of the mall is the food court. All different smells in the air walking in—some burger joint in one corner, a pizza place, I think even some Mediterranean food just moved in here not that long ago. I also go to Salvatores on The Go when I eat here. It's a cute little Italian-to-go place that has pastas, gnocchi and meatballs buffet-style. It's not homemade, but it's pretty damn good.

Waiting at a table in the food court for Rebecca to show, I pull out my journal. The noise that surrounds is a dull roar of chatter. The table I choose for today is incredibly uneven, which will be interesting to write on to say the least. The pattern on the tables is some nineties swirl with highlighter colors, and a blue background they set on. I know Dr. Psych will be upset with me if I don't log in at least one day this week. While I wait for Rebecca to show, I'll write about what's been going on the last week, and hopefully that will be sufficient to get me out of the doghouse.

Just about to put pen to paper, and in walks Rebecca. Time to shop.

I throw my journal back in my bag, zip up quickly and head in her direction.

I can always catch up on writing later, right?

Rushing myself over to the store she's heading into, Rebecca must not have seen me sitting down, because she doesn't wait for me to catch up. My hair is in my face, and I'm slumped over my journal. I am not far behind her, but she is already in the store by the time I catch up. The music playing is like a nightclub, LED lights very unflattering on the skin, and most of the employees have caked-on faces. As soon as Rebecca walks in, one employee rushes right over to her to assist. The employee already has a few outfits picked out for her, like a personal fashion assistant—knowing her style and that she is here every Friday around the same time. Rebecca tries them on and comes back on with a sour face. She must not have liked any of them.

For over an hour after that, she is in the store searching through endless crop tops, skin-tight shorts, pants and shoes I couldn't even imagine being able to walk in. Rebecca tries on about fifteen outfits in the timeframe, all with an array of different shoes. She finally decides that she is getting the jeans with some purposeful tears in them, a white crop-top and a pair of gladiator sandals. Makes me feel a bit self conscious about my apparel. Basically, it's a t-shirt with some logo I don't recognize and jeans with sneakers for me.

In the summer, when it gets hot, I do wear shorts, but typically the bermuda ones, not the short show-my-cheeks-off ones.

The employee that didn't get the outfit pick suggests a pair of fake gold dangle earrings to match her necklace and new gladiator sandals. I figure Rebecca is going to tell her no, but she must feel bad about not choosing one of her outfits because she says yes. The employee, extremely excited, rings her items in. They exchange a small conversation about what the outfit is for. The fake excitement between the two nauseates me, so I walk out of the store and into the mall for the next part of shopping.

Rebecca cashes out with her gold platinum credit card, and heads towards the pretzel place in the middle of the mall. She orders a pretzel twist with a small cup of cheese and a lemonade, and I snag the last cup of pretzel bites. She sits quietly, no doubt planning for the party this weekend. It's at an old farm that is no longer in use. The farm is less than a mile from my house. There is a corn field that cuts it off from the road. The road is a dead-end anyways. There is nothing but forest that surrounds the area, quiet and secluded—the perfect place for a party. The last party spot, an abandoned home on the edge of the woods was blown up a few months ago.After the police raided they haven't been back to that spot, so it was time that a new one was established.

Before we leave, Rebecca heads into a fancy dress store. Is it possible she still hasn't found a dress that she likes when we are so close to prom? It's three weeks away.

She talks to the women at the cashier station and is left to wait. I realize she must have custom ordered a dress and it has arrived. She will have to try it on to make sure that it fits and the measurements are perfect, although anything she wears will look drop dead gorgeous anyways.

Oh, I am so excited to see what she looks like in it.

I feel honored to be able to see her first in her custom-made gown. The cashier reappears with another woman who has a dress wrapped up on a hanger in her hand. The women put the dress in the dressing room, leaving the door open and inviting Rebecca to enter.

After she disappears into a dressing room, the anticipation of seeing her in the dress makes it feel like she has been in there forever. Finally re-appearing really only moments later— *Wow. Just* wow!

Rebecca's gown is a baby-blue shade that has a corset top, sweetheart neckline, and a big ball gown bottom. The entire dress is lined in gemstones, and crystals shining off the light like diamonds. Cinderella is the only thing that comes to mind while I am staring at her in the picturesque moment. I am in complete awe of her beauty. I have my camera, so I snap a quick picture for the memory book I started. She is looking in the mirror holding her face in complete shock at the beauty this dress possesses. She hugs the woman that brought the dress out. The woman then points to her feet, asking what shoes she will be wearing. She wants to be sure that the dress is the proper length with the shoes Rebecca will be wearing on the big night.

Rebecca says she hasn't picked out any shoes yet to match her dress, and the woman holds her face in shock. The woman waltzes right over the desk, grabs a book and rushes back to Rebecca's side. She hands Rebecca the book, and shows her a page from it, pointing out a few pairs that will go with her outfit. Rebecca shakes her head "yes" to one pair. The shoes must be in the store, and in her size.

What a lucky day.

The woman walks swiftly into the back room swiftly, almost dancing on her feet when she re-appears in the room and opens the shoe box in the most revealing fashion. Rebecca looks as though she has tears in her eyes; she is so happy they have her size in the shoes she was looking at. To my surprise, they are a pair of clear heels mimicking the glass slips of Cinderella. How fitting, and such a match to our Disney-themed prom. I am so incredibly happy for her at this moment. She is a vision.

I wonder if Rebecca is upset, she hasn't said much as we have been walking through the stores. If she wanted to talk about it she would just start in on what's going on, which she obviously doesn't right now. Which is also fair she is trying to enjoy the moments of getting ready for prom. I hope she's ok.

Leaving the dress shop Rebecca heads over to the bookstore. I know she does the library for school research, but I am unaware that she reads just for the fun of it. Seems highly out of character; maybe there are some magazines there that she likes to pick up.

Surprised yet again by her today, she heads into the non-fiction section of the bookstore. Looking around in the criminal history documentaries. Rebecca picks up some of the classics—Jeffery Dahmer, Ted Bundy and Zodiac. I can't help but think she is really just picking up books for a class, but that can't be true, because what class would she need these for?

There is a simple answer for that—there isn't one.

What an odd collection for her to be reading. After a few moments, still holding these books in her hands, Rebecca looks over at the coffee shop and decides that she needs a caramel fix. Most people, after reading the back of those books, would have lost their appetite for any food or drink, but she seems unphased. I don't drink coffee. It makes me wiry, and I can't shut off or function. I browse through the non-fiction section myself, and pick up something on Elizabeth Bathory. I have a collection at my house on true crime.

I should see if Rebecca would like to read any of those.

Rebecca grabs her caramel frozen coffee, and it's off to the next store. There is only one other stop she hasn't made yet, and that's the jewelry store kiosk. It's back on the other side of the mall towards the way out. Rebecca only stops for a few minutes this time around, not purchasing anything, just browsing. Chit chat with the employee, who I believe goes to our school, but I can't place her name. We both look at our watches at the same time, and realize we really should be going. The crowds start after work—about five thirty—and it's no longer fun to walk around when it's wall-to-wall people and we are bumping shoulders with everyone we come into contact with.

It's time to leave, but we will see each other tomorrow at the game while I'm taking pictures of everyone and she is cheering on the team. Of course, I'll have a chance to see her tomorrow night at the big bash if I can manage to sneak out of the house and make my way there. That didn't work out so well the last time for me; however, I have a pretty good plan for this go around.

I definitely want to be there, so it better work.

My mom is waiting for me outside the mall, ready to take me home. I open the passenger side door and hop into the seat, snap my seatbelt on and look at her to tell her I am ready.

My mom stares at my book and then at me.

"Interesting choice you have there." Her eyebrows are raised. I am not sure whether she is going to ask a question, or is just stating how she feels.

"Yeah, I thought it could go with my collection. I remember some movie with her in it, but I don't think I have read the book about her." I shrug my shoulders with my reply, as if it's no big deal that I admire historical serial killers.

"I have read it," My mom says. "It's gruesome, but interesting for sure. She believed the fountain of youth was living inside young children's blood, and that she could harness it by draining and bathing in it."

My jaw literally drops.

"What? You think I have never had a morbid curiosity? I used to be just like you. Although I would have come to the mall for clothes, not for a book." And there's the jab for the day. I almost thought this was a good conversation we had going.

"I am just shocked that you would have read something like this. I know we have read some things in common, but I didn't think my crime section was up your alley. I don't really need any clothes. I have more than enough to choose from." Hoping this answer is a cute response to make her leave the subject of my wardrobe alone.

"Right. Well, I guess we still surprise each other then." This will be the end of the conversation, because she can no longer pick anything apart the way she had intended to get me to change my style, or lack thereof.

The rest of the ride is quiet. When we arrived home, she had picked up Chinese for the night. She must be working on something important to have Chinese. It's one of my favorites, but she prefers to cook to save money, as well as it makes her feel better that she still cooks me dinner. I do enjoy her cooking—it tastes better than most restaurants.

I throw my back pack on the vacant chair in the corner of the kitchen table as we walk through the door. My mom walks over to the refrigerator after closing and locking the door behind her, and grabs a bottle of red wine off the top shelf. Now I know she has had a long day; I almost feel bad for shutting her up in the car. That may have been her way of reaching out instead of being snide. I advance to the kitchen and grab her a glass before she has had the chance to turn around. I nudged my head to tell her to sit in an attempt to reconnect with her. We exchange smiles. I pour her a glass and we both sit at the table with our take-out containers.

"I know you felt attacked in the car about your clothes, and that's why you shut me down. I'm sorry. I shouldn't do that to you. I had a really bad day at the office, and a tough case that just wrapped up."

Wow. it must have been a day to have her apologize.

"It's okay, Mom. I'm sorry that I tried to get you to stop talking. That wasn't right. Do you want to talk about your day?"

She smiles at me, stands up and grabs a second glass for wine from the cupboard. She pours the wine into the glass and sets it in front of me.

"Yes, I would. If you're willing to listen."

I nod my head to let her know I am all ears for her at this moment, and I smile. This feels pretty good to me—that she wants to open up. We sit, and I listen to her talk about the tough case she has been through all week. I clean up the take-out containers from dinner, wash the wine glasses in the sink, kiss my mom on the forehead and head to my room with my things.

Long day ahead of me tomorrow.

CHAPTER 5

Saturday, Two Days Ago

Saturday mornings often start the same way. I get up, look around the tornado space that I call my room, tell myself I should probably clean this, and then jump in the shower. This Saturday morning is a Dad visit morning. I have had pretty limited time with him recently. He moved, and with our schedules, I can only see him for a few hours instead of the day like I used to.

The game is at four so I have to be back for that. Rebecca would be so disappointed if I didn't make it back.

In the shower and getting ready, I keep it pretty quiet, hearing only the beads of water running from out of the shower head, feeling the warmth on my skin. Most people listen to music or sing or even talk to themselves. I like the quiet—silence to live inside my thoughts. The steam covers the room as I turn off the water and grab my towel, barely able to see an inch from my face. Reminds me of that movie where the killer is in the bathroom waiting in the steam cloud in the bathroom. The actress can't see him, it's so thick. She doesn't know what's coming, and next thing you know, she's being slashed open by some giant knife. I jump from the shower to the door as quickly as a flash, swing open the door to let some of the steam out and wipe the mirror down with the corner of my towel. My eyes scan the room vigorously while I stand still.

Nope. No killer here.

I audibly exhale. Close to a panic attack about an imaginary killer.

Staring into the mirror at only myself. Brushing my hair is always a chore, so I choose to do that last. Makes me envious of Rebecca's blonde locks that have a perfect beach wave. Throw my hair in a towel, dress myself in some Plain Jane jeans and a t-shirt, put on some mascara and then attempt to put a brush through my red tight curls that are complete knots. Most mornings I don't take a shower, the amount of effort it takes to get myself together after a shower is too much on a school day. I usually wash my face and throw my hair up. I don't wear any other makeup except mascara so that's easy enough to take off during my night shower and re-apply in the mornings.

Saturdays have a very different routine due to the amount of time I have. I am up at the same time as if I was going to school, and have plenty of time before I can coax my mom into leaving. Finally, getting my curls to untangle and lay as nice as they'll get, I throw a clip in to get the pieces out of my face and decide to go downstairs.

I don't bring anything with me to visit Dad—just myself—so it's time to see if Mom is ready to head out. Down the stairs, she is sitting at the kitchen table with a large coffee mug and papers spread across the table—probably the case she is working on for the week.

"Mom, are you ready to go?"

Not even looking up, she says, "Yeah, yeah. Are you sure you want to go?"

I want to say, "Why wouldn't I want to go? Because you don't want to drive me? You don't want to see his face today?" Getting ready to go into panic, I breathe in and out deeply.

"Yes, mom. Can we go?"

She doesn't answer me.

"Like now?" I snap.

"Yes! I said that we could. Let's get to the car, then. You know it's over an hour away."

I roll my eyes at her response, knowing damn well how far away it is, but she *has* to bring it up every Saturday we go to visit.

Arriving in front of a building that must have seventy rooms inside. It is massive. Built like an old castle, pointy decorative roof tops, with statues all around on the lawn. Dad hasn't had a job in awhile, so having a room to himself is a nice feature given his situation. At his old place, he shared a room with three other people, but he was only twenty minutes away so I could visit more often. If I map it out the right way, I probably can catch the bus here, provided my mom says that I can.

The building looks like the front of my school—cobblestone steps and large wooden doors. It was built sometime in the 1900's, and remodeled some time ago, although you can still see some of the original features, like the large stone art work carved in the walls that they didn't cover.

Walking right through the door, it's eerily cold in this building. Unwelcoming. The walls are mostly white with some combination of grays in other rooms. The smell in the lounge and entry area is mixed with stale cigarettes and bleach from trying to keep the area some form of clean. It's quiet in the entry all the way to the lounge area, where I start to hear indistinct chatter amongst the residents, the TV from whatever program they are collectively watching, and periodic yells from the winner in Gin Rummy.

Through a hallway and to an elevator, I press the up button, and we wait for the ding. A gentleman in just a hospital style gown walks past, talking to himself about what sounds like a story about a cricket. Or maybe he is talking to a cricket.

My mom and I, both wide eyed, look at one another and then back to the elevator, not engaging with the gentleman. The elevator arrives and we jump right in. Thank goodness, we are alone. A ding for each of the floors, watching the numbers count, at the third floor the doors open and we hop off. My dad's room has a window that views the rear of the building, so he might not know we have arrived.

He hasn't been here long, so we don't know any of his neighbors to say "hello" to. We just walk past the other residents, nodding politely and smiling. The hallway is the hangout area where the residents talk and play cards and smoke cigarettes, even though they have the recreation lounge on the first floor of the building.

Room 326.

The door is already open, so I knock on the off-white metal frame that surrounds the doorway and say "hello" so as not to startle my dad.

The room is empty, considering our house and how many decorations we have on the walls. Dad has everything he needs, it's just very plain. The floor is a green-blue tile, the walls are lined with a white tile that meets the white stipple ceiling. He has a bed in the far-left corner—twin-size is my guess—metal black frame and bars for the foot board and head board. There is a table next to his bed with a lamp and Bible open to some passage, his glasses resting on the open page. The only other piece of furniture in the room is a chair. A gray microfiber rocking chair that faces the window, where he is sitting now. This must have been a donated chair, because there are cigarette holes all over it and my dad doesn't smoke.

He turns to the door, a smile on his face from ear to ear. "Hi sweet pea."

He leaps from his chair to sit on his bed, and I swivel his rocking chair so we can see each other face to face. My mom has already disappeared from the doorway; she usually comes back upstairs to get me when it's time to leave.

My dad is relatively tall—at least six feet. He has sandy blonde hair that he keeps long enough that it falls into his face a lot. When he stresses out, he runs his long finger through it to brush it back. He only wears glasses for reading, and he has a ton of wrinkles on his face. He looks much older than my mom does. Although, I imagine his skincare routine here isn't as top notch as hers. He's a very thin, long individual, and his eyes are the same green as mine. When he smiles, he has dimples that sink into his cheeks, and lines that hold his smile into place. His smile is the most warmhearted thing I have ever seen, an instant good mood when I see it.

"How is school going for you? What are you learning about?"

"Well, we have started using solvents in Chemistry. History we are learning about the Spanish-American war. Math is always the same, and in English we are reading "To Kill *a Mockingbird*." I think I spit that out without taking a breath.

"That sounds like a caseload. Sounds like it is going well. I'm glad." He pauses. "Your mom didn't want to even say "hello"? Is she working on a big case?"

"Oh, yeah. She is totally distracted lately, must have gotten a phone call when I walked in," I lied. "How are you doing? This new place is pretty interesting. I love the artwork." I changed the subject quickly.

"It's okay. I hate being further away because I can't see you as often, but it is nicer than the last one. The artwork is nice..." He pauses for a moment to look around his room as if I was talking about it here.

The next two hours go on like this, just back and forth catching up on every little thing we possibly can. Seems like only minutes have passed when there is a knock on the molding. A man stands with a yellow food tray in his hand.

"Time for lunch. I didn't know you had a visitor. I can come back."

"No, that's okay," I say, swiveling the chair back to face the window. "It's time for me to go anyway."

My mom is standing behind the gentleman, motioning for me to come to her.

"Dad, enjoy your lunch. What service for them to bring it right to you! I love you, and I'll see you in a few weeks." Giving him a kiss on the cheek, I turn towards the door, and walk around the gentleman with the tray. "See you in a few weeks."

"Never soon enough Sweet Pea. Drive home safe," winking with his reply.

On the way home, my mom drills me with questions about what we talked about. She always seems scared that I am going to divulge some secret information, or tell him too much about what she has going on.

One of the only times we talk in the car, or really at all.

"Did he ask about me? Did he say he is doing okay there? Did he ask about my work? Did you guys talk about the house? Did he ask you about what we have been doing? What did he mean, 'never soon enough'?" Rapid fire without a chance to answer in between.

"Mom, we talked about school, the weather, how he's doing and what I have been up to. Nothing else." Simple answer to sum it all up into one.

I watch the physical sign of relief drop over her face, to her shoulders, and into her stomach. I can't really decide what she is worried about. We live a pretty uninteresting life, and my most interesting parts—I can't just tell my dad, "Hey I have been sneaking out to party with the school teams and cheer squad and hanging with Rebecca every chance I can get." Those are pieces I have to leave out. He's still my dad, no matter his situation.

Home for less than five minutes, I pack up my camera and stuff that I need for the game, and shuffle my way back to the car. Mom and I drive into town, right back to our normal form of silence on the ride there. She drops me off in front of the school. She never comes in or watches the game. She hasn't had any reason to engage with my school activities for awhile. The only time she really ever has was that time on restriction, when she followed my every waking move. Even then, it was forced agony for her, having to take part in my menial day to day. She stuck to it, though. I'll give her credit for that. Past week one, I figured she would have given up, provided what an inconvenience it was.

"I have too much work to do. I'll see you at five." Like clockwork, the same phrase, so I close the door before she's even able to finish the sentence, and go to the gym.

Snapping pictures of the cheerleaders and the basketball players as they score. Watching intently, fixated on Rebecca as she stares down Nate, cheering him through every pass. While taking pictures of the athletes, I am rarely sitting. I move from our side to the opponent's, in and out of the bleachers. I get my steps in for the day just walking back and forth to get the best shots I can get. Once a week I post them on the school website after I go through edits, and save the best ones for the yearbook, of course. One of the other students does a monthly magazine through the school, and he uses some of my photos when we win, which is rare.

Yet another uneventful game. We lose, but even with the loss, Nate runs over like it's the best day of his life, picks up Rebecca at her hips, spins her around and gives her a kiss.

He turns towards me. His smile falls, and he advances in my direction.

In a panic I clam up,.I am counting down in my head in an attempt not to collapse to the floor. My feet frozen to the gym's sleek floor like cement blocks are strapped to them. Standing there frozen in time, my shoulders at my ears, my hands sweaty and gripping my camera as tight as I can against my chest without breaking it.

Nate looks right down to me, finger in my face and says "You better back off and leave her alone. I mean it you freak. I have seen you, and I'll be watching." Hearing the squeak of his sneakers as he swiftly turns around back to face Rebecca. He jogs over to her, grabs her hand and with a smile picks her up. Within a flash, they are all out of sight.

The janitor is here mopping the floor with some machine similar to a Zamboni, but much smaller. The lights are dim, and the bleachers are pushed back toward the walls to allow the entire floor to be shown.

How long have I been standing here?

Why haven't I moved yet?

I haven't been able to move from the same spot that I was standing in when Nate so viciously confronted me. Coming to, I look down to see if there really is cement on my feet that's not allowing me to move. Obviously, that's not the case. There isn't anything there.

What was that though?

Why would he say that to me?

I feel so disoriented about the interaction with Nate, He doesn't understand our friendship. I guess I can't blame him for that. Sometimes I wish Rebecca and I could have our friendship out in the open, but I'm still happy to have her friendship in our own little way. Feels more sacred.

Still shaken, I finally mustered the courage to move, and go to meet my mom at the car outside. I'm sure she is furious with me.

I have left her waiting outside. I am not even sure for how long. I haven't looked at a clock since the game ended.

She doesn't say a word as I open the car door or on the way home. Everything must be okay; she can't be that mad, or she would have at least yelled when I stepped up to the car door.

I think about telling her about Nate and what he said to me about Rebecca. Instead, I stay silent. I am not ready to divulge my friendship with her or share any of the information I have been secretly guarding. If I tell her about Nate, I won't have a choice but to release the rest. There is no context without knowing Rebecca and I have been hanging out for months, something that she knows nothing about.

So that's where I'll leave it.

We arrive at home, and I go directly to my room, thinking about the party at the abandoned farm. It's not a far walk. I realize that I still want to go, even with Nate going off. I can still see my friend Rebecca, and maybe get some clarification. Maybe I can get her alone so we can talk about opening up our friendship. Let people know that we have been friends and hanging out for a while. That way this doesn't have to happen again.

I go down the stairs and to the kitchen, and open the freezer door. My mom must have bought Rocky Road ice cream this time. Reaching up to grab two bowls from the cupboard, the freezer door starts to beep from being open too long. I snag two spoons from the drawer, scoop out two scoops each into our bowls, throw the ice cream back in the freezer to stop that annoying tone, and join my mom on the couch. Handing her the bowl with her favorite chocolate curls sprinkled on top.

We sit in silence. Within minutes of finishing her ice cream, she is completely passed out. Her work hanging from her hand as she lays on the edge of the couch, I take the papers and lay them on the glass coffee table, drape a throw blanket over her from the headrest on the couch and head to my room.

It's go time!

I scramble through my room as quickly as I can. Everything is always everywhere, but somehow, I know where everything is. My black MTV hoodie from the back of the chair sitting by the window where I usually read. Black sweatpants, one leg sticking out from under my bed. Slip on my sneakers—one by my dresser and one in my bathroom. I grab my backpack from the edge of my bed.

Down the stairs for the hundredth time today, and scurry out the front door, quietly closing it while watching the couch from the window, making sure not to disturb my mother's peaceful sleep.

I'm going to this party!

CHAPTER 6

Saturday Night, Two Days Ago

Spring nights in my neighborhood are quiet. School is still in-session, so parents get their kids to bed early, as they have already eaten dinner and packed in for the night.

We live outside of town in a nice little community—no busy roads, roar of traffic, light pollution, restaurants or bars that are close. Crickets are just starting to buzz. My feet *pat, pat, pat* on the pavement below. The full moon hangs in the sky like a round lit-up Christmas ornament. Every single star in the night sky is visible. No breeze or movement to the air around. It's not cold, and the air is fresh but warm against my cheeks.

There is something therapeutic about walking at night. The anxiety of sneaking out of my house completely flushes away within the first fifty feet of walking. The excitement of going to the party is setting in. It feels like it's my birthday, waiting for the singing to conclude to blow out the candles.

The old farm is a little over a mile from my house. I arrived within a half hour of leaving my house. Taking in the giant corn stalks that stand before me. They stand straight at attention like the soldiers at the Queen's gate. Looking up there is an orange-yellow haze in the very near distance. They must have started the bonfire already.

I wonder if everyone is already here. I embark on my mission to get through the stalks and join my classmates. I wonder as I am walking through if Nate and Rebecca have already arrived, and if they came together.

Will I have a chance to ask Rebecca why Nate has an issue with me?

Will I get her away from the group to ask if everything is alright with us?

I extend my hands in front of my face so that I don't get hit as I'm walking through the stalks. Walking slowly through the uncut corn is key—the leaves would cut my skin to shreds if I ran. It's pretty dark in the corn, but in front of me, I can start to see the flames burning taller than I have ever seen. The team brought some pallets to set on fire. Illuminating the space in front of me, sparks drift upward, embers below glowing red-hot.

Coming to the end of the corn walk, I can see a few pick-up trucks with their tailgates down sitting around the giant flames. Four legs per truck kicking from off the end of each tailgate with the exception of one truck that has eight. A red Ford F-150 is pulled closest to the fire, and I can just make out Rebecca and Nate sitting in the back.

I recognize the sandals she has on before I recognize her face. Rebecca bought them on our mall trip yesterday evening.

Laughing and carrying-on, everyone has a red plastic cup in their hands. Starting the party early I wonder what they are drinking, but more than likely, it's bottom-shelf cheap alcohol that someone could score earlier in the week.

I hear a ruffle from behind me. Someone else is coming in from my freshly walked path, but who?

"Boo."

"Oh my god, Raymond!" I nearly jumped out of my sneakers ready to run. He definitely got me.

"It is I." He bows, saying with a chuckle.

Raymond isn't really my friend, but we are both outcasts in most circumstances. At the parties, it gives me someone to talk to. Neither of us can drive. We both walk, and usually he beats me. This is my first time out since I was caught. Raymond must have been coming alone. I am somehow relieved to see him, just to have someone to stand with, knowing no one else will talk to me.

He's nerdy, has a great sense of humor but I have seen him be down right nasty to people that tick him off. I try not to ever cross that path.

"Have you been here or are you just getting here?" I'm asking to assess the situation.

"Just got here. You wanna snag a drink?" He uses his elbow to jab mine a few times while winking.

"Yes, of course. Pour me one?" I ask politely. I didn't bring anything to drink, so I'm hoping he will share.

"You got it, Kid." He speaks to me like he's from another time. "What were you looking at when I got here? Seems like something had you in its grasp?"

"Oh, it was nothing really..."

Do I tell him?

"Well, earlier today, Nate and I had a weird interaction, so I was wondering if Rebecca and Nate were already together tonight. I was hoping to ask her about it." My teeth are grinding together. I'm not sure how he will reply to that.

"Oh, that? Yeah, I saw some of that. What's his problem?" His reply shocks me a little. Who else was watching?

"I'm not sure. The hope was to gain some clarity. Should we go closer to the fire?"

Raymond nods in approval. Just as we are about to make an appearance from the corn, I hear Rebecca yell from the back of the pick-up truck. I look in her direction, and she slams her cup down at Nate. She has just done a shot, and is laughing and yelling in excitement. Jumping off the tailgate, she heads to the woods behind the gray barn that stands forty feet tall, unused for the last twenty or so years.

Raymond pours the drink from his bag into a green plastic cup. I'm thinking to myself, W*hy green and not red*? I brush off the thought, because who cares? We each take a swig out of the brand-new bottle, shivers run down my spine and my mouth starts to salivate. We giggle, "cheers" and take a drink, which has very little mixer. The alcohol instantly warms my chest and stings my throat at the same time.

Staring towards the direction of the barn to see if I can spot Rebecca. The beauty of this old structure is taken for granted. In the daylight, the gray color from the aged wood looks like fresh ash from a fire has been rubbed on it. The ten foot sliding barn doors are intact, with large white wooden X's on the center of each door. Forest-green roof shingles have fallen over time and lie on all sides, only a few left from the wind storms we have had. The roof has mostly held on for how long it has been abandoned. On the inside, the building is empty but has so much character, and without a doubt could tell a million stories about the animals and people who once lived here. They must have had horses here at some point, because four stalls built on the inside line of the walkway, and the outline of hay that has molded and deteriorated into the cement is still present.

"Where do you think she went?" Raymond's puzzled expression matches my own.

"Maybe she has pee." Shrugging my shoulders, as if her leaving by herself into the woods to pee is a reasonable explanation.

Raymond and I take another shot.

Holding my cup, taking sips of this terrible liquid that must be Raymond's choice of tequila, Rebecca still hasn't come back. No one has stopped laughing or exchanging stories to see where she has run to.

Why is no one worried?

Looking around, Nate is still in his truck bed, and no one else is missing—still the same number of legs hanging down.

Maybe time hasn't passed like I think?

Is she waiting for me?

I should go find her. What if she got hurt or can't find her way back through the wilderness? I let Raymond know I am going to retrieve her and make sure she is alright; Rebecca shouldn't have gone out there alone. Only a flashlight, alone and drinking seems like a bad mix.

We agree to meet back here after I have found Rebecca, and I head through the corn over to the forest.

I don't scare easily, but something about this forest gives me goosebumps. It's dark—not just night time dark, but pitch-black dark. Dense trees cover the path that is usually illuminated by the moonlight. The trees are thick, intertwined with one another at the tops, and the bottoms have made pathways.

I read about this place in Japan—Aokigahara Forest—they call it the "suicide forest". The forest was grown on lava from the eruption of Mt. Fiji some time ago. The forest is dense, and the lava bedrock causes absorption of the sound all around, so the silence is like nothing you have ever felt before.

I feel like I'm there right now—I can't hear or see anything.

No rustling of leaves, no wind, no animals scurrying about, just...blank.

Peering through the woods to try and catch a glimpse of Rebecca's flashlight. Still there is nothing.

I descend deeper into the abyss, and all of sudden, I catch a faint sound of Rebecca crying. I want to rush over to her, but I am not quite sure which direction she is in.

I plug my ears and let them go quickly trying to hit the reset button.

That seems to have worked. I can hear my name. Does she know I am here to find her?

Is she in trouble?

Why would she come out here by herself to begin with?

"Hannah! Hannah!" I can hear her cries in the distance.

"Hannah, this isn't funny. Come on, please. Please"

"Hannah, let's go."

"Hannah, get me out of here!" Her crying is taking over any other noise in my head.

I am on my side, no longer on my feet. I am on the ground. Lying on the damp soil, I can feel the moisture soaking through my clothes. There isn't any grass, it's unable to grow with the lack of sunlight throughout the woods—just soil, and in the distance some swamp spots.

My head pressed against the dirt, I am listening for Rebecca. I can hear her, faintly, but she is there. Trying to form the strength to scream out in hope that anyone can hear me. Rebecca, Nate, anyone. But nothing comes out.

What was in that drink Raymond gave me?

Something isn't right. I close my eyes.

Kaboom!

Sounds like someone exploding a firework right beside my ear. I can still hear the laughter, but it is so far away from me. I'm getting progressively dizzy; I feel like I'm falling fast, but I'm already on the ground, so there is nowhere to fall. Like in a dream, when I realize I'm falling, and suddenly wake in bed with a jump.

Kaboom!

Another earth-shaking movement from above this time. My entire body goes into a convulsion like I am having a seizure.

And just then, my mother's voice...

"Hannah!"

"Hannah! Can you hear me?"

"Wake up Hannah. It's almost time to go"

My eyes open suddenly, I'm in my room. I rub my eyes and give myself a quick pinch. Nope I'm really here in my room and my mom is walking me up. I am grasping for thought trying to place how I woke up here in bed . Terrified that what I was dreaming might have been real.

What has happened? Why can't I remember coming home from the bonfire?

Where was Rebecca?

What was with that dream?

I shudder, wiping the goosebumps on my arms trying to shake it off.

Today's off to a bad start...

CHAPTER 7

Present

*W*hat the hell was that?

My rage flushes over me like a wave smashing to the shore of the beach.

Tink, tink.

There it is again.

I stand up slowly from my bed, pillow in hand. I advance to the window slowly and cautiously, not sure what awaits me on the other side, letting the clench of my fist release and dropping the pillow on the floor. I am on the second story of my house. How could someone be knocking?

As I peer through the windowpane, there stands Raymond on the grass below. Unlatching the locks on my window to push it open as quietly as I can so my mother downstairs doesn't hear me. The smallest creak lets out as I get it open, just enough to speak out. I quickly turn my head to the door to be sure I don't hear her footsteps coming up. I wait for a moment, staring towards the stair railing. She must not have heard anything; I turned back to the window.

"What are you doing here?" I whisper, trying not to be heard. It's a nice night—the windows downstairs might be open.

"Checking in on you. You okay, Kid?" His genuine concern is appreciated at this moment. Finally, someone that cares about what I am going through.

"Yeah, I am ok. I can't talk for long. My mom is right downstairs. She might be able to hear you."

"Meet me at the old farm when she goes to bed. Let's find this girl!" He smiles from ear to ear, as always.

Thankful that someone wants to help me, I reply, "Yes, let's do it. I'll meet you there! Give me an hour."

Not caring about the hurricane that is now my room, I snatch my backpack from the ground, set it on the top of the stairs and head down the steps, peeking to see where my mom is. I catch just a glimpse of her on the couch, sitting with files in hand, staring at sheets of paper with small writing. I try not to look excited as I walk through the living room and into the kitchen. I am holding my shoulders in a slump, and a miserable look on my face.

I feel like a terrible actor. I fear she will notice I am faking still being upset and call me out.

She pays no mind to me as I reach the kitchen. I turn back to see if she has even looked up, and still, in the same position she sits. I go to the freezer, and grab the new mint chocolate chip ice cream that sits in the usual ice cream spot. Set it on the counter quietly, and pivot my feet to grab two bowls. Still trying to be sly about grabbing ice cream, I open the drawer softly, grab two spoons, scoop out two scoops into each bowl and top my mom's ice cream with the chocolate curls. Walk over to the couch where she doesn't look up and says, "Does this mean you are okay?"

No words needed. I hand her the bowl, we eat and minutes later, nothing but *zzz*'s.

Just before I am about to put a blanket on her from on the top of the couch as I did before, a folder under her stack catches my eye. "Re" are the only letters that appear—this folder is a different color than the others. It's green, which is missing person cases. She has only ever had a few of these in all the time she has been at the firm. Most of those cases had something to do with classmates of mine, or people we have come into contact with. Carefully and quietly, I slip the folder out of the pile, without disrupting the ones above or below. I can read the whole name on the side now.

Rebecca.

Rebecca's file is in my mom's office?

Is she helping the investigation for the disappearance?

I open the folder, and Rebecca's picture is affixed to the upper right corner with a paperclip. I rub my thumb across the picture. It is the same as the one the woman was holding on the picket sign in front of the school. My eyes scan the inside pages *left to right, left to right* as fast as I can skim through the words and comprehend. If I get caught looking at this folder or any of her work, I am in some deep shit.

She didn't want me to see this file in her possession. When I walked over with the bowls, she shoved it under the others to conceal it. The names that are listed as suspects are the students who were called into the office today during chemistry. The same students that were at the bonfire on Saturday. Each student the alibis for the next and their presence being accounted for. No one could account for where Rebecca had gone just that she wasn't any one of them at the time. She was last seen walking into the woods to go to the bathroom, and never returned. I flip through the pages to see if anything extreme pops out. Current pictures of all the students, with their statements written by some investigator.

Is my mom going to take the defense for this case?

Is she looking at the case because it's Rebecca?

Nothing jumps off the pages to seem suspicious or catch my attention until I see Nate's statement against me. My name pops off the page from his statement. Along with something about the garbage can.

My mom swings her hand down as it drops from the couch, almost slamming her face into the side. I drop the file and grab her head to stop her from getting hurt. She doesn't wake. I set her head down softly onto the side of the couch and move her hand so it's resting by her knees instead of dangling. I bend down to see the file is all over the floor, and shuffle the pages back into order.

Thank God they are labeled with page numbers.

Now that I have scared myself half to death from almost being caught, I slip the file under the others back to its original position with just the letter "Re" being visible. Fly up the steps, grab my bag and back down out the door without a sound. Hopefully Raymond is still waiting for me and hasn't given up on helping me search for Rebecca. He seemed eager to help, but it has been much more than an hour with my distraction of the file.

I cannot grasp why Nate has it out for me.

This walk isn't therapeutic like it was Saturday night. The wind is whipping through the trees; the clouds cover the night sky. The air has a chill, and there are no crickets in the background tonight. I'm slightly jogging towards the dead-end road and the corn field trying to not be seen by anyone. With the investigation still at large, I don't want anyone to be suspicious of us going to the old farm.

I find myself in front of the corn field at warp speed. Examining the corn field before I enter, the howling wind blowing the corn stalks to the side. I didn't notice on Saturday that in the center of the field stands a scarecrow with a dim light above it. Paranoia is setting in...

What if there are cameras that are in the scarecrow or the light? What if that wasn't there on Saturday?

Could the police really just have installed this system to catch any-one trying to enter the old farm or the woods?

I walk through the corn, arriving at the old barn. I can see the fire pit from Saturday night. I walk over to where everyone was parked. Getting close enough to the fire pit to witness the tire treads that remain from the parked trucks. The grass was wet then, but not wet enough to leave ruts. The tire treads that are left are barely visible without a light shining on them. They must have extinguished the fire once they realized that Rebecca was gone. There are plenty of pallet edges and pieces that are charred, but hardly burnt through. The group doesn't strike me as the type to leave the party until the fire is out, unless the police arrive or something goes terribly wrong.

Turning around to see the statuesque barn towering over me even from this distance still so large. I admire this building. Peaceful... *Snap out of it, Hannah. Time to go into the forest beyond the barn.* I have yet to see any sign of Raymond either. He must have left. I did leave him hanging for a lot longer than intended.

Navigating through the trees, some are so close together I have to turn to the side to get through them. I see an opening ahead of me. Approaching the opening, I duck my way between two trees that have fallen against each other. The soil below me is soft, and even through my sneakers, I feel like I am walking on air. It's loose and moist, large clumps crumb with ease as I step on them. I come into the clearing and see footprints scattered all over the area. The police have been in here day and night since Rebecca was reported missing, and this being her last known whereabouts.

The dirt has been disturbed in one area. It looks like someone took a broom to it. Drag marks coming from further into the woods. I follow their breadcrumb trail until they stop in front of a tree. Curious—more shuffle marks. Where the drag marks stop, a tree stands tall—thick red oak. I would have to wrap my arms around it twice just to touch my fingers on the other side. It must stand sixty feet tall past the tops of the trees around it. Admiring the sheer size of this tree, I see a glitter where the roots begin. The shine of the object has hit the moonlight in the perfect way. I reach down to grab the object from the loose soil. I hold the object in my hand.

Is that a flashlight?

It has to be the police. They are still searching the area to find Rebecca. They have walked all over these woods. I can see the footprints without touching the drag marks or even coming close enough to disrupt them. I am bent down, kneeling to retrieve the object that I now possess. I jump to my feet as quickly and inconspicuous as I possibly can and get myself ready to run.

There is something else sticking out of the ground that catches my attention.

Wood?

Why is there wood sticking out of the ground?

Looks like a piece of wood from the barn.

I hear one of the police officers' shouts to the other. "Hey, I think I see something moving over there!"

"Go check it out, but be careful. Could be a bear."

That's my cue to move my ass.

Clenching the item in my clammy fist, and like a flash of lightning, I run through the trees hoping I can retrace my steps without injuring myself. I sure hope that Raymond did leave and isn't still out here. I wouldn't want him to get caught just because I took so long. I ran past the barn, not stopping to admire its beauty once again. I check the flashlights behind me as I look back to see if I still need to run. They are far enough away, but I don't want to take the chance they may catch me out here, and especially before I can look at what's in my hand. This won't look good for me.

I throw my hood up and over my face. I don't want to cut myself up running through the corn. Then everyone will know where I have been this evening.

Once I have cleared the corn, I slow myself down and take a few really deep breaths. Running is not my strong suit, but the adrenaline in my system is still so high that I have a headache.

My house in my sight, I decide I can stop on the side of the road for a moment and take a breath. I start to walk again and almost forget that I have the object still clenched in my fist. I hold my hand up investigating the shiny object I found next to the tree.

It's a necklace—a gold butterfly pendant with a diamond in the center.

I can feel my eyes starting to well up. It's Rebecca's necklace.

CHAPTER 8

Six Months Ago

It's Rebecca's birthday. I tell my mom that I am going to the library in town and that I'll be okay to take the bus. Rebecca and I just started to hang out, and I'm not ready for Rebecca to meet my mom or to hear any of my life story just yet. Plus, my mom and Dr. Psych get super involved in my social life when I start to talk to someone. I had a crush on someone last year and made the mistake of bringing it up in my weekly meeting. Dr. Psych told my mom, and all of the sudden, we are having sex talks, attempts at shopping trips and an interest in how we met and how serious things are. Literally a childish crush turned into an invasion of adults. I stopped talking about him completely, and the invasion faded. Not trying to relive that nightmare either. I spend a decent amount of time in the library and take the bus system often, so this isn't out of my normal.

This plan works as long as I am seen at the library first. The librarian not only knows me by name, but knows my mother just as well. As long as I am seen there first, I can sneak out and head to Rebecca's. The librarian will think I have lost myself somewhere in the deep seeds of the building and won't know any difference, but can assure my mother I have arrived.

The bus stop is only a few houses down from mine. I insert my headphones in each ear, turn on Pachelbel's *Canon in D Minor*, and trot to the stop. I arrive at the bus shelter, and find a safe and secure spot to plant myself while I wait. Encased in a set of plexiglass walls, the sun is shining through, giving me warmth. There's a door on either side of the bus shelter. I decide to sit in the middle to have the best reflection of the light on my skin, pulling more of my freckles to the surface.

The bus arrives. I wait for a moment to allow any passengers to get off, and seeing no one, I walk up the stairs, scan my pass and find an empty seat. The buses aren't like school buses—more like travel buses. The seats are individuals next to one another. The smell isn't much better than a school bus—some bad hygiene, some smells of groceries from moms shopping for the weekends. Gum under the seats, kids' sticky handprints all over the armrests. It's bearable for only a fifteen minute ride to the library.

The library is a simple building, like a Tardis. Brown brick with a black flat roof, simple glass doors and a little display window on the front of the building that shows the top-pick reads of the week.

As I walk in, the smell of book pages floods my nose. That smell is intoxicating. I spent so many of my nights after school and weekends in this building. The books line the walls; roller-ladders everywhere to be able to grab the books off the top shelves. Shelving units from floor to ceiling flow through the center of the library front to back.

The librarian's desk is directly in the center of the building. Large and round like an orchestra pit. I approach the desk to say "hello". She knows my voice, and doesn't even look up from the book she is currently devouring. Her name is Mrs. Stein. She's an older woman, with white hair and glasses always wearing long skirts and a knitted cardigan over her shirts. She has wrinkle lines around her mouth that look like she doesn't spend a lot of time smiling. They match the furrow lines in her forehead. When she looks up, they flatten. She raises only her eyes above her glasses, and not the rest of her face.

I have made my presence known; now, to go get lost in the library and slip out the back. There is a back door that is never locked that I can slip back in once I have come back to keep my cover story. As long as I get back within library hours, I'll be golden. Walking past the fiction, non-fiction and towards the horror section, sucking in the smell of the books as I walk past the shelves.

Reminded as I walk past the tables that this is where Rebecca and I had met—in the non-fiction section—only a few weeks ago. She was so incredibly nice to me. Rebecca could have told me to get lost that day or even that she had the book first and I could check it out when she was done. That's what any of her friends would have done. Instead, she insisted that we work on the project together so we could get it done at the same time. Who would have ever guessed I could bond with someone over some history project?

The only ones in the library that day reading and writing our papers, we spent hours together. I asked if she needed a ride from my mom, and she motioned towards her house that was visible from the back of the library, letting me know she was okay to walk.

I smile as I walk past our table and keep myself moving.

Eerie that the back door of the library is where they keep all the books about ghost stories and serial killers. I look at a few of the new arrivals, peek up front to the desk through the aisles, and Mrs. Stein is still enthralled in whatever she had in her hand when I arrived. Probably some gushy romance novel with explicit scenes that I would never consider touching. *Yuck.* I shake off the image I just implanted in my head, put the book back in the middle of the "New Arrival Horror Novels", and advance to the door. Slipping through, holding the door with just my fingertips to not let it slam shut.

There is a hill behind the library that leads right to Rebecca's neighborhood.

After about a ten minute walk behind the library and up the hill, I am in front of Rebecca's. Standing in front of me is an amazing statuesque, architectural dream. White siding with black shutters, a wraparound porch on the first and second floor, with a round gazebo off to the left-hand side. The gazebo looks like someone ripped a page from a picture book, with four perfectly set places on a wicker table with four chairs, a vase in the middle with some wildflowers including one big sunflower in the center. Every tree in the yard is trimmed to perfection, and bushes cut into little circles that look like I could pick them up and put them on an ice cream cone.

No action in the front—I can hear all the voices coming from the backyard. Walking around the mansion and not encountering a single person on my way around the house. The backyard is just as awe-inspiring. In-ground pool bigger than my living room and kitchen combined. A water slide and diving board affixed at the deep end. I didn't realize she had a pool. I didn't bring a suit with me. Tables and chairs surround the pool area each with their own umbrellas to cover from the sun. Barbecue cooking on the grill, the scent making me salivate. I don't know any of her relatives or any of the other girls here. Looking around in the most lost way, I find myself an open seat near the edge of the pool and just observe. There isn't anyone sitting at this table. I am far enough away from the main event that I doubt I will be joining, so I can make myself comfortable.

People with money seem to celebrate the same way as the rest of us, no different rituals at birthday parties. Arrive, chit chat with everyone, catch up, eat, sing happy birthday and have some cake. Of course, the ritual everyone always waits for is presents. The gifts are much more lavish though. At this time, everyone is sitting down, small chatter amongst them but dulled down. Chairs turned towards Rebecca and her parents, waiting patiently for her to start ripping through the paper.

The only difference between this birthday and mine is there are so many people here to celebrate her birthday. It's usually just me and mom at the house. We have my favorite dinner of homemade sauce and gnocchis—one of the only times a year my mom cooks. We have gifts, but only a few, and I sit on the living room floor, tear them open and disappear to my room to be with my things. Not that I am jealous at this moment. It's just interesting to watch a different way of celebration.

Rebecca starts to go through each gift, thanking the guest who brought them as she opens. She isn't ripping through the paper like I do; she is delicately tearing each edge to reveal the gift or box the gift was in. She runs through a pile of gifts and cards, things for her room, new clothes and handbags to match—nothing of great importance but she is grateful all the same. She opens what everyone thinks is her last gift, everyone cheers for her and stands up ready to rush over and sing "happy birthday" so she can blow out the candles. Her mom looks at her dad with a wink. Her dad runs up the stairs into the house and appears quickly with a small box in hand.

Rebecca opens the box and everyone inches their way closer to her to see it. It's hard for me to see around everyone, even being tall I can't manage to tower over the crowd in front. Her dad comes over and puts it around her neck and I can finally see what it is.

A beautiful golden butterfly necklace. An ornate butterfly pendant with diamond-cut texturing that catches the light. An oval-shaped diamond that makes the body of the butterfly in the center. Attached to a Singapore gold chain.

After receiving it, I don't think I ever saw her without it.

Tonight there is a football game, so the birthday celebration has to be over in time for everyone to get themselves ready for the game. Which gives me plenty of time to make it to the library before it closes. Looking down at my watch, I'm still in the clear. I grab my things and leave the party around the house and down the hill. I leave earlier than Rebecca and her friends; I need some practice shots of the team to put into the yearbook. Getting to the library, I open the back door, sweating and hoping that no one's face meets mine as I walk through. No one there, I slide through and sit down for a moment, looking at my watch to see what time I have to catch the bus. I hear my mom's voice coming from the front of the library.

How long has she been here?

I hear her laugh and realize I am still okay. I start to walk towards the front of the library, arriving at the desk.

I ask, "What's so funny?"

"Oh, nothing, just shooting the breeze. Are you ready?" my mom asks.

"I told you I would be fine taking the bus." My tone unsettles me.

"I know. The game starts soon and I thought if you were still here, I would pick you up to bring you to the school. You said you would be home an hour ago. You have practice shots to take."

Damn, I did say that to her. The flaw in my otherwise flawless plan.

"I brought your camera; I'll take you up to the school." Her voice is almost chipper. I wonder what she has been up to, but my wonder is clouded by the irritation that she was in my room.

"Thanks. Let's go then. Goodbye Mrs. Stein. See you soon."

"Goodbye, Hannah. Be nice to your mother," she says quietly enough for just me to hear.

With my back turned away from her, I roll my eyes and throw my hand in the air to wave goodbye.

I arrived at the field before the opposing team, the sun still hung in the sky low enough that if I reached out I could touch it. The air is cooler than it was just only an hour ago, but only enough for a long-sleeve shirt. Once we all start to move, I'll sweat, and I won't even notice the temperature change. I reach the gate that surrounds the field to keep the spectators separate from the game. Rivertown Ravens displayed on the field, freshly-painted white yard lines and markers outlined on the field. Outside of the fenced-in field are bleachers—home side with a white and purple bleacher box for the officials to sit in to yell out what is happening on the field through the speakers. The opposing side has a smaller set of bleachers with no box, but still speakers on each side to hear the announcements and happenings while the game is in play. A digital screen towering at the end of the farthest field goal that will show the score as the game proceeds. Large poles extend from multiple points around the field that will later illuminate the as the sun begins to set.

As the players are practicing, I sift through my bag and make sure I have all my batteries, lenses and spare SD card just in case I need it. When I don't pack my own camera supplies, it's hard to know if I have everything I will need. The team comes running from the locker area on the far-left side, not yet in full gear because they are just doing runs and stretches to warm up. We have a little less than an hour before the bleachers are filled. The opposing team takes the field to warm up. The game is shortly to follow.

Camera ready, standing on the locker room entry to grab photos of the team coming out. When we win everyone likes to see their excited faces in the beginning of the game, especially since by the end, the team is exhausted. The cheerleaders with their purple, white and silver pom-poms yelling and pumping up the crowd to greet the home team. The announcer says the starting players, and I write down the names as each one comes out and greets their cheer bunny. Cheer bunnies are cheerleaders assigned to each player to help them workout, stay on track for the game and motivate them to win. They obtain so many stains for the field markers—the grass and the collision into one another—but every game, they start off with stark white uniforms. A silver lining around the purple, and black raven in the center.

The whole crowd is on their feet, cheering the team on and yelling to their favorite players. Noise makers sound off so that I can barely make out what the crowd is actually saying, but the team yells back and throws their hands in the air regardless. I take a seat until the game actually begins. Every home game, they introduce the seniors and the top players from the previous week, and to be fair they do the same for the visiting team. I have the shots I need of the seniors in action for the year, so I sit quietly with camera in hand and a bottle of water in the other.

The concessions smells of popcorn and pizza that the boosters sell to raise money for the team's travel, new equipment and maintenance for the field. The smell is intoxicating. I am starving, but I'll have time at halftime to grab a bite. The games are a giant pull for the town; the Ravens have gone undefeated the last two years. Everyone comes to see them win. Football is significantly better than our basketball team—only some of the players play both—and I'm sad to see we will lose so many of our best players this coming year, but nice to have them go out with a bang.

Grabbing some money shots during the first half of the game, the score at halftime is fourteen to twenty-four. The cheer squad comes out, performs the halftime dance and stunt routine, and riles the crowd back up. I slip away to grab a slice of pizza, much needed nourishment and another bottle of water. I sit at a picnic table alone and just observe the other students with their parents. The way they talk about the game sounds like the NFL playoffs, the parents equally involved with the season. I almost admire that they so freely speak about their lives—who is dating who, and what the daily gossip happens to be.

Why does it flow so freely for these guys and not for my own life?

Would it hurt to include my mom in anything that is going on?

Really though, would she even entertain my high school interactions?

My thoughts are interrupted by a cheering roar from the crowd as the girls finish and the team rejoins the game.

Rebecca is in the center of the cheerleaders' grouping. Being the captain, she earned that spot. I stand at the front of the bleachers so I can take photos of the girls while they face the audience to cheer on the defense and ask us to join in. The cheer ends, and they have three small pyramids with Rebecca in the center. The stadium lights are on now, and they shimmer off her golden locks in the photos.

I envy her.

Throwing herself out there at every turn, she is engulfed in the spotlight so often it must be second nature for her.

The last quarter is just about over. Everyone is sitting on the edge of their seat. Nervous that we might actually take a loss for this one, the score is too close for comfort. Of course, in the last two minutes of the final quarter, the Ravens make a comeback and beat the opposing team. Thirty-eight to thirty-five. The crowd in the home bleachers comes out of their seats in excitement ready to celebrate the win. The buzzer goes off a minute later, and the cheerleaders rush onto the field. The team players from the side lines jumping up and down in elation. Within minutes, the team has said "good game" to the visiting team, and the bleachers have emptied into the fenced area.

Everyone hugging and kissing their kids and friends. While they celebrate on the field, I dip through the traffic jam in hopes to say congratulations to Rebecca and the team. She has already gone into the center with the team, and there is no use for me to fight my way in. We can talk about it later.

Gather my camera bag and head over to the parking lot assuming my mom is already sitting there idle and impatiently waiting. I have to get home to make a plan for later this evening. My mom usually falls asleep on the couch, so sneaking out is no easy task.

This is only the beginning of the team's celebration for the evening, and I want to make it.

CHAPTER 9

Six Months Ago

A t home, I put on a pair of black sweatpants and a Raven sweatshirt to show my support of our win. I grab my backpack, throw it over my shoulder, and head to the stairs. Put my backpack on the top step and shuffle down the stairs. My mom is in her usual spot on the couch, surrounded by files and working on her latest case. This week happens to be taking a toll on her. The case is about a young girl. She has been asking me weird questions about how teens communicate in order to piece her defense together. Tonight, she must have been working extra hard because she had already fallen asleep when I got down the stairs. I grab a throw from the top of the couch to cover her. She switches sides so I hold my breath with the assumption I have just woken her. Settling down within a few seconds and no more movement, I know that she isn't getting up. I turn back around and jump for joy up the stairs quietly, snag my bag, head down and out the door.

Tonight's celebration is at an abandoned house that happens to be not far from the roundabout in my cul-de-sac. I leave the door and start walking to the right. The air chilled more than it was before. It's crisp and stings ever so slightly as I breathe in. I can see my breath as I exhale. Good thing I was smart enough to pack a jacket into my backpack just in case.

I have just left my neighborhood, reaching the brush that outlines the woods behind a neighbor's house. I don't think I have ever had an interaction with the people who live here—not even sure they would know who I am if they saw my face or happened to be awake. Once in the woods and out of clear view, I take my backpack off my shoulders, set it on the ground to take my coat out. I place it on, zip it up to my chin to keep it from getting cold and put the hood on over my hair. Shoving my miscellaneous items back in my backpack, I throw it back over my shoulders to continue my walk.

The signs of abandonment are very clear upon arrival. The state of disarray tells me this house has been here in this condition for some time. None of the windows have glass—they have all been blown out either by weather or kids passing through. The house has no color and was built completely from wood, not siding and plaster like modern-day houses. The doorway is still there, but pushed in and tilted so slightly, I can no longer gain access from that entry point. Vines have grown over the building on one side, covering it like they have been painted on. A tree growing from one of the second story windows, I would guess that it starts on the inside of the house growing outward to find the light. The back side of the house has fallen in, the wood from the roof and sides caved into the middle of the room.

The windows are large enough to just walk through. There is only a few feet from the ground to the sill. As I gaze through one of the windows, I can see the team is already here and have started to set up. One of the seniors brought tables, and another brought folding chairs. They are starting to unload, setting the tables in the middle of the room for a beer pong tournament and another off to the side to hold the booze. The cheerleaders start to file in and take up a chair so they can watch the festivities while consuming their own fruity mix drinks in their red cups. The murmurs of chatting are suddenly drowned by the music that comes from the stereo placed in one of the corners of the room. The sounds echo from the emptiness.

Rebecca and the girls are sitting directly in front of me, whispering to one another about each of the players and who they find attractive or who is available. I don't have anything to add to these aspects. I know who is a couple, but rarely am included in the daily gossip. Nate keeps looking over at Rebecca. She was assigned as his bunny this year. At one point, he winks in her direction. She giggles, and her and the girls continue their jibber jabber. A few of the couples are in the distance, not paying attention to the beer pong game or the others. Making out, talking close and basically on top of each other. I have never seen Rebecca or her sidekicks act that way in school at games or anywhere in public, so I assume they are single. I couldn't imagine that she would behave that way even if she did. The flashlights the team brought only cast light upon some of the room, corners and sills are mostly dark.

I take in the space as I look around.

The room is covered in cobwebs in every corner, and stretched across every window other than the ones disturbed by us walking through. Debris and dust all over the floor, holes where the floorboards have finally given out from being in the elements for so long. I have found a seat on one of the sills in the front corner of the room, away from the main event. The chairs are all facing the middle where the floor seems to be solid. The beer pong game will be the main event at this gathering. As everyone grabs their drinks and their seats, my thoughts start to wonder.

I close my eyes and try to imagine what this house looked like when it wasn't in such chaos.

I imagine a family--mom, dad and kid—sitting on the couch, enjoying some hot cocoa on a cold night, watching the fire burn to keep the heat. Telling stories about the day, the dad a farmer in overalls, dirt covering his clothing from working in the field all day. The mother in a modest ankle length dress, who has been home cooking and cleaning and teaching her child the duties of the day. Home schooling in their time was not an oddity, and the mother took the responsibility of instruction in reading and writing. The child is in a pair of jeans and a long sleeve shirt that are hand-me-downs from a cousin or other family member. This room is small but perfect for a family to enjoy each other's company in. The tea kettle on the fireplace steams and screams that it's ready to be served. Perfect end to an evening.

"Yooooooo!"

Just like that, I am snapped back to the party. Someone from the team is playing beer pong double bounce, and everyone is in utter excitement. The drinks are flowing and the party is starting to get louder between the noise of the stereo and the chatter. As the voices of everyone in the room get louder, someone keeps turning up the stereo, overpowering the volume of the laughing. From behind me, there is a rustle in the brushes. Unsure what that could be—I didn't bring my own flashlight because the moon in the sky was enough to light my way here. This is the first party I have snuck out for so I'm not sure what could have made that noise, but I have a terrible gut feeling.

I fall back from the window sill, turning my legs as I fall to land on my feet. My sneakers hit the dirt, and I decided to bolt into the woods towards my house. Once I am out of sight from the party, I turn back quickly to take a glance, and I see the flashlights hitting the side of the house where the roof has fallen in. As they hit the windows like cockroaches, the whole football and cheerleading team flee the scene. Jumping through the windows, leaving everything behind and going to their vehicles to get out of dodge. Some have parked further away for an easy escape route. Running in so many different directions, I am almost positive that everyone has gotten away. I see the faintest glimpse of Rebecca's face as Nate throws his coat over her and shoos her towards the opposite direction I am in.

Like Northern Lights, the sky is lit with blue and red, and police officers come from all directions surrounding the house. The onset of panic is imminent. I can feel it in my chest and ears. I don't have time to think, let alone run a countdown in my head to slow the panic or my breathing. I can't get caught, not on my first round. This was fun, and I want to be able to come back.

I desperately need to get back to my house before the commotion wakes my mom from her slumber. Praying that there aren't any police officers coming from the woods in front of me. That would be worse than her just being awake. My first time sneaking out to a party, there is alcohol everywhere, even though I didn't drink, and the cops bring me home to my front stoop. Thankfully there isn't anything in front of me—the police officers must know that no one is parked at the end of the cul-de-sac. There are houses all the way around, so it would be rather hard to be incognito that way. The sirens will echo in the neighborhood just beyond the trees in no time, which could get me caught by the neighbors. Even if they don't know who I am right now, they could blow me in.

Running as fast as my feet will carry me to my front door, my heart beating out of my chest. I am out of breath, my eyes fixated on just getting to the door before my mom wakes up. My brain is running faster than my feet with all of the possible scenarios I am about to walk into. There will be hell to pay if she has been woken up and I am not in that house. Panting, sweat dripping down my brow, the chill in the air has faded. My body is so hot, like sitting in a sauna for the past twenty minutes with my jacket on. My feet hurt from pounding the pavement so hard. I haven't eaten since that slice of pizza at the game, and I'm a tad dizzy.

Finally, I reach for the door knob, turning it slowly to not wake my mom. She has to be in the same spot on the couch. I open the door slowly, pull my head up to look up the stairs and her eyes are directly at mine. Her foot tapping the ground, arms crossed, death stare directly through my eyes like laser beams. Her brow is furrowed, mouth turned in a deep frown.

Well, I'm toast.

CHAPTER 10

Three Months Ago

A few months have gone, but not quickly enough. I am finally off my restrictions. Boy, did I get my mom riled up more than I have ever seen. The last time I saw her like that was the last fight that she had with my dad before he left. She has been disappointed in me, and even slightly angry with me, but never like that.

Of course, I didn't tell her I was at a party. I told her I was walking through the cornfields in the opposite direction over by the old abandoned barn. Taking night pictures was my excuse, and when I got there, I realized I left my night shot lenses at the house. I tell her I couldn't even get the images I wanted, trying to appeal to any sense of empathy I could gain in that moment. Accomplishing nothing, she couldn't have cared less about what I was doing—she was furious. I could have been out meeting the Pope, and it would have changed nothing.

She grounded me from going anywhere but school and home. She sat at every game that I had to take pictures for the school yearbook, as well as drove me to the library, which was confined to her schedule and when she could take me. After a few months of sitting and staring at my popcorn -style ceiling, I swear I know how the lady in that short story feels, "The Yellow Wallpaper". I was slowly becoming one with the walls. Thankfully, it's over, just before I pop into complete insanity and start to eat my own face. All that would do is piss her off more anyways.

I am happy to be back to our normal and off to school with some freedom. I wouldn't be surprised if she planted some tracking device in my shoes though.

This is an important week, and I can't have her hovering over my every move. I want to be a part of the stage crew for the drama club. The spots are limited, and I know she wouldn't transport me to and from, nevertheless sit in the auditorium for hours after work and weekends. We will be working on this for the next several months, and a piece of me wonders if she planned this so that I would have something to occupy my idle time.

I had mentioned the drama club and the production a few times in a small conversation with her.

Was she actually listening to me?

Auditions are after school today—stage hands don't have to attend, but it's encouraged. Rebecca said that she was going to try out for the lead. She is so amazingly talented. There is no way that she won't nail it. The school has decided that we are doing "Beauty and the Beast" this year as our production. I actually contemplated trying out, but I doubt I would get anything but a backup role. I can't carry a tune in a bucket, as far as dancing goes. I can do "the Carlton" and that's about where it ends.

Usually walking through the hallways at the end of the day is a madhouse, everyone scurrying to the buses at the loop or to their cars to get out of this place. Today with the auditions, a line has formed through the auditorium doors, everyone shuffling in to find a seat next to their friends. Only the front section is open for the auditions. The balcony section– a few stairs upward but at a slight elevation to see over the lower level—is taped off. The ceilings in the auditorium are cathedral, and there is an opening in the ceiling where the lighting instruments and sound equipment sits. Catwalks running in either direction so someone can move the lights or speakers to make the optimal show. Most of the electronics are on remotes in the box at the very top of the theater seating, but every now and then, someone from the crew may have to make a manual adjustment. The walls are a very plain tan color, matching the carpet, the seats a velvet-red like my favorite cake, as well as the laneways to the seating. Very majestic place to be in with optimal acoustics. The sound echoes from the stage to your ears.

Several students take the stage all the way from "Little Town, It's a Quiet Village" to "Be Our Guest". All of them do well until Rebecca steals the limelight. No one could hold a candle to Rebecca when she's on the stage. Her blonde locks touching her shoulders, a beautiful butterfly necklace hanging at the top of her v-neck shirt. Her voice is that of angels coming right from her puffy lips. sings through Belle's song and then is asked to sing "Something There". They love her, the audience applauding with mouths open, hanging on her every note, whistling as she finishes her audition. The choir teaches in awe of how she controls her voice so well. There is no competition. She has it in the bag. Everyone here knows Rebecca has won the lead role of Belle. Another two hours or so, we watch student after student audition. No one else even attempts the lead after Rebecca, but we still need a Beast and Gaston, and where would we be without Cogsworth and Lumiere?

The auditions finish, everyone turning to each other in congratulatory bliss, even though no one finds out until tomorrow. We all exit through the back doors, and head to the late buses that have been kept for us. Once I arrive at home, I see my mom isn't here yet. I grab some lemonade quickly from the fridge and head to my room. I am excited to see the list tomorrow. I grab my headphones, throw them on, turn on my side and I'm out like a light. I can hear the sound of Rebecca's voice in my sleep, so sweet and in perfect pitch. The notes visible from her mouth coming out and wrapping around me as I lose myself in the pleasant and soothing ambience.

BEEP BEEP BEEP.

BEEP BEEP BEEP.

Interrupted by my incredibly annoying alarm clock. It's impossible to be morning. I haven't been asleep long enough to hear the alarm blaring. My eyes open and I realize it is in fact morning and time to get myself moving.

The list of casting is posted near the office on a bulletin board that has all the news for the week. All of the students who auditioned yesterday evening are huddled around the list searching for their names and the part that is attached. Some walk away with frowns even though they got a part, because it wasn't the one they wanted, or it's a backup role. Some walk away cheering and screaming with delight that they were placed in the role they so desperately wanted. We hosted several shows, so some parts were split between two people. The role of the Beast split between two kids on Tuesday, Wednesday, Thursday, and the other Friday and Saturday, with a matinee and evening show on Saturday. We have about two months to prepare for the show, and the practices will be constant and hard work, but it always comes together perfectly. Being on stage crew, I make the sets and move them from one scene to another, so the list doesn't matter much to me. I will take a look when everyone has stopped gathering so closely.

Rebecca steps up with a group of her squad following close behind. Holding each other's hands tightly as if this is a life-or-death moment for each and every one of them. Everyone in front of her parts like the Red Sea to allow her to take a glance at the list uninterrupted. Her face lights up instantly. She got the lead for all of the shows, with only an understudy. She can perform every night as long as she feels well enough to do so.

I slink past the group, under my breath utter the word "congratulations" and keep it moving. I am not sure that she heard me, but I am sure that a celebration will happen later after their first rehearsal has commenced. I will do anything to make even a glimpse of that celebration.

Every night for the next two months is spent at the school. Even though the stage crew doesn't seem like the best job to have, we are the eyes and ears of the shows. We are a student run-organization, and we all have jobs and responsibilities that make it happen. If one of us isn't in the right spot or misses a cue, the cohesive play looks like children in a sandbox playing pretend. In the beginning stages of setting up the show, we have to build, paint and create so the audience feels like they are really living the production. We all have our areas we specialize in—for some, it's audio, lighting, or backstage. I enjoy the backstage portion, dressed in complete black to not be seen during lights out. When we layout the set, we place glow in the dark tape on the floors to set the props in the right position for the upcoming scene, color coded to each set.

My favorite scene of the play is "Be Our Guest". It's the simplest set up, with only a table and a chair. The dishes are laid out on the table and glued down so that they don't move as we roll it to and from the stage. The props are only out for half of the scene, so two stage crew members sit in the table hidden by a cloth. Halfway through the song, they jump out and bring the table backstage to allow the dancing silverware room to move about the stage. The colors of the lights in this scene are like being at a rave; streams of color come from all directions.

While working on the stage crew, I've had conversations with plenty of the other students, but never gained any real connection with anyone. We came to the last show of the performances. Rebecca is on stage with Beast. They close the scene, and now Gaston comes on and takes the stage for the next several minutes.

When Rebecca is backstage, she starts to get dressed for her next appearance. Her wig falls, slips off her head while she is changing and drops to the floor. One of the stage hands accidently kicks it as they walk past. Rebecca grabs her head, and instantly her expression shows that she is aware the wig is missing. There isn't a backup wig purchased because she is the only Belle. Everyone is on hands and knees within seconds of it going missing, searching under every prop and set piece, turning over tables and checking the show curtains.

I see the brown wig with a blue bow resting on the back of it. It's under one of the prop tables. I run over as fast as I can, and compile my thoughts to swipe it up quickly, before anyone else can take the credit for averting the wig crisis. I dust off the back of the wig, attempting not to disrupt the bow. The dust falls off the wig, onto my shoes and the ground below, making me think we should probably do a good clean back here.

I approach Rebecca, snagging the hair pins on the prop table as I walk to her.

"I found it. Do you want me to help put it back on?" Shy and timid, but a comforting smile on my face, her expression settles and she returns my smile.

"You are a lifesaver. Could you imagine the last few scenes with a blonde Belle?" She smiles. "Yes, I would love some help. Do you know how to pin it?"

Delighted that she is going to let me help, I nod my head "yes" and she flips around abruptly, bending down so her head is at my waist. I adjust Rebecca's cap that has her blonde curls wrapped in it, pushing her soft displaced pieces back into the cap. I carefully slid the wig onto her head, and started to place two hairpins by the nape of her neck, another two on either side of her head behind her ears and the last two in the front of her head above her eyebrows. She slides her hands above the temples and gives a slight shake to the wig, just enough to make sure she can move about on the stage, dance and sing without losing the hair piece once more on stage. That would be embarrassment to the highest degree.

"Thank you. I owe you one!" She winks at me, and it's time for her to return to the stage.

The curtain closes on the show as the Beast and Rebecca dance to "Tale As Old As Time". Months worth of work rolled into a few days and the finale. Wrapped up in just a few short hours. The curtain reopens to allow the cast to take the final bows as they call the names from the box, congratulating each one with applause that echoes throughout the entire auditorium. Rebecca comes to the front of the stage for her finale call, and roaring from the audience gets louder with clapping whistles and excitement.

Nate comes rushing from the front row onto the stage and joins Rebecca. Everyone gets quiet as he grabs a mic to speak. Nate is tall with an athletic build, and it's obvious he really takes care of himself. He must be in the gym daily keeping himself in shape. His hair is dark brown and long in the front. It just about touches his eyes. He's always throwing his head to the side to clear his eyesight. Nate's skin is year-round tan, and his eyes are dark chocolate brown to match his hair. Nate is always dressed like he is going to a job interview. I guess that's considered a preppy look. Polo shirts in very light colors—today happens to be a very light shade of blue. Khaki pants and dress shoes, similar to loafers in my opinion. A gold braided chain around his neck. If we voted for things like "class clown" and "longest hair", he would get "best dressed" by a mile.

The entire audience is in a still frozen moment in time, hanging onto their seats and waiting for Nate to make his announcement. He looks at the audience and back to Rebecca with mic in hand, parts of his lips that are a simple perky shape, his bottom lip a tad pouty but shiny like he has on lip gloss.

"I know this isn't the best timing, but Rebecca did an amazing job tonight. Am I right, everyone?"

The whole crowd cheers.

"Rebecca, will you go out with me?"

She wraps her arms around his neck, brings him in, and he picks her off his feet as they kiss and he swings her around in a circle. He puts her down, and her arms rest at his waist. Nate brings the mic to his lips once more.

"Is that a yes?" he asks with a charming smile. That damn smile that no one could say "no" to.

"Yes!" She smiles back at him, and they pull in for a kiss. He holds his hand to the side and drops the mic holding onto Rebecca. The entire auditorium is on their feet cheering and whistling for them.

The curtain closes.

CHAPTER 11

It's Thursday, five full days of the agony waiting for some news. They haven't found Rebecca or any real sign of her. Some disturbed dirt and footprints that they haven't been able to match to anyone. No clothes, no belongings, no trace—just vanished into thin air.

They have searched the woods, multiple student's homes. All of the students who were initially called during chemistry on Monday. The police have continued to camp out in the principal's office. They haven't called anyone down since Monday, but they have kept a close eye on a few. The school is a complete lock down throughout the day. We can't leave for any reason without a parent there to sign us out.

Nate has been absolutely nuts, acting irrationally and talking to all the students that were at the bonfire, trying to figure out what happened from the moment Rebecca left his tailgate to the moment she didn't come back. I know he has been out in the woods searching for some sign that she is still out there.

He threatened me in passing on Tuesday morning. We were walking in opposite directions through the hall, and he jammed his fist in the air at me saying, "If I find out you had anything to do with this, freak, I'll end you."

A teammate of his grabbed his shoulders and walked him forward before someone heard him threaten some random student in the hall. The cops have been on his tail since Monday, watching his every move, assuming he had something to do with Rebecca's disappearance. They caught him in the cornfield Tuesday night searching for her himself, and they brought him to the station for questioning. He doesn't look like he has showered or changed his clothes in days. Large bags under his eyes, he must not be sleeping either. I am surprised he has even been in school at all. Rebecca's parents have stood by him the whole time; however, the police assume that this was a relationship issue gone wrong. They have been just waiting for him to slip up or make a move.

The feel in the halls walking each day from class to class is ominous. No chatter amongst the others, everyone patiently waiting for the next name to be called to the office or the next person to be escorted out by the police. If they are still hanging around here, they must have a suspect. Similar to a scary movie and there is a serial killer on the loose in the town.

We have a curfew in effect, and my mom has jumped to a new level of annoying with that. I can't go anywhere alone, like I am being punished for Rebecca missing. I am confined to my house, on top of that I am forced to sit at the table to do my work. I think she hopes I will give her information on what is going on at school. She doesn't understand that I am just not ready to talk yet.

<u>Wednesday Night</u>

Last night when we arrived home, I sat at the table while my mom cooked dinner, and finished my work in silence. Once she was done, she served me a plate of pasta, and we ate only the sound of the forks hitting the plates, until she looked up and spoke.

"Any news?"

"No, they haven't found anything yet." I reply in a sad tone.

"How have you been feeling? I noticed while cleaning your bathroom your meds were not on the counter. I found the empty bottle in the garbage." Her response has a touch of curiosity.

"I flushed them on Monday." I know that she is aware of that, after my outburst I had when no one seemed to care about finding Rebecca.

"Yes, I thought that was how it went. I refilled them and put them on the counter for you. After we eat, be sure to go up and take them. And maybe shower?"

So now we are worried about my personal hygiene as well as my medication. I roll my eyes as I think about how idiotic this sounds to me when Rebecca's parents are sitting at a table right now worried they will never see their daughter again.

"You got it," I say as sarcastically as I can express.

"I hope you mean that. You're going to see Dr. Psych tomorrow before school. Between your outburst on Monday, all the commotion at school and Rebecca missing, I think it best you see her more than once a week for now." She's staring through me, waiting for me to reply, but really what is there to say?

"Okay."

I push my chair behind me to stand up, grab my plate and take it to the sink. When I turn on the water, I find myself zoning a bit. Thinking back to Saturday night, finding Rebecca in the woods searching for a place to use the restroom where she wasn't in sight of any of the party-goers. The way she turned to look at me in utter shock that I was behind her.

"Hannah, what are you doing out here?"

"Hannah!" my mom yells.

"What?" I yell back.

I look down, and water is pouring out of the sink onto my shirt and pants. I flip the faucet off, and reach my hand in to pull the plug.

I look down at my pants and let out a laugh at how much water I managed to get on me and now the floor.

"Sorry, I wasn't paying attention. I guess I can skip the shower," I say with a chuckle in my voice.

"Very funny. Help me mop this up and then go get yourself cleaned up."

I do so and collect my things from the table, throw them in my bag that's sitting on the chair next to my spot and head up the stairs. As I touch the railing to walk up one foot on the first step.

"Don't forget your meds!" She's yelling as if I have already made it up the stairs and out of ear shot to hear her.

I roll my eyes and walk into my room. Stare at the meds on the counter and lay down in my bed for the night.

<u>Thursday Morning</u>

My schedule seems off kilter. It's Thursday, but getting up to go to Dr. Psych makes it feel like it should be Monday. The days have all meshed together anyhow with the shock of everything that is happening around me. I chose a different type of clothing today. Instead of my usual t-shirt with some logo and a distressed pair of jeans, today I grab a light blue v-neck and a bootcut pair of jeans. I plan to wear my cowboy boots that I hardly touch. My mom bought them for me when I was horseback riding one summer, and they have sat in the closet since then. I french braid my hair and tie it back out of my face which takes me about fifteen minutes longer than my usual ponytail. As I walk myself down the stairs to join my mom in the car, I think to myself, *Today will be the day there is some news.*

Arriving at Dr. Psych's office, walking through the white french doors with that eerie feeling of deja-vu.

"Hi Han, Hi Trish."

The receptionist standing at attention as we walk through the door, like she has been waiting for this moment since she arrived in the office this morning. Per usual, my mom heads right to the desk, smiley and happy, talking to the receptionist about where she got her new purse and this shopping spot she found. Unlike usual, I grab a seat in one of the brown chairs and actually manage to sit all the way down. Dr. Psych is generally ready for me as we come in, and I never truly take in the atmosphere around the office. There are a bunch of abstract paintings on the walls all by the same artist—something Dali. One of the paintings is what my brain feels like most days, these melting clocks lying all over the place in a desert. A dry empty space that has time slipping away from it with the sun beating down. Even medicated, I never feel normal or like I function like everyone else. My thoughts travel and wander all over the place. I can never keep track of them the way I want to. I do see the value in my medication.

I don't lose loops of time. How can this painting make me feel so guilty for not taking my medicine? Is that why it's hanging there?

"Good morning, Hannah," Dr. Psych calls from her doorway.

I grab my backpack from the ground and make my way into her room. Sitting on my favorite chair, I start to sway back and forth.So relaxing.

"I have heard this has been a tough week for you. Care to share some of your feelings on what has been going on?" Her question resonates in my head. Do I have the choice not to respond?

"Well, where do I begin? I didn't know that Rebecca was missing until I was leaving school Monday. I felt as though my mother may have been hiding that information given she just found out that her and I were friends that morning. When I found out that she was the missing girl, I was saddened in a way I can't explain. My heart dropped, and the pit of my stomach emptied. I am sure my mom told you I was at the party where Rebecca went missing. I don't have any information. I have lost the memory of that night into Monday morning and coming to see you." I gasp for air as I spit all of it out in one breath.

"Okay, Hannah, good. I am glad you are being honest with me. I talked with your mom about this. I don't think she was hiding information from you. I think she found out at a similar time and came home to talk with you about it. She told me she found you in the dark at the kitchen table just sitting there. I know this doesn't help the situation, but I hope it eases your mind a bit that she wasn't withholding from you. I am sorry that your friend is missing and that you feel so terribly about it. Can you tell me what you remember from the party that night or anything afterwards?"

Should I really tell her exactly what I remember up until I heard Rebecca's voice calling for me?

Do I hold that information back?

Is it possible that she is trying to figure out if I was the last person to see her?

Am I a suspect?

Here it goes...

"I showed up to the party by myself, and Raymond was there shortly after. We had a few drinks, and I watched Rebecca head into the woods. So much time had passed that I was worried, so I ventured into the woods to find her. I thought I heard her voice, but I must have been mistaken, because next thing I knew, I woke up at home in bed after my dream Monday morning."

Well that sounds insane. Way to go Hannah...

"I want to thank you for coming forward. I am struggling to understand how you don't have any memory for almost 48 full hours. Hearing Rebecca's voice was that in the dream, or did she actually talk to you when you found her. And who is Raymond?"

"It's hard for me to tell if it was a dream or if it was real. Raymond is some kid that is an outcast, similar to myself. We don't hang out, he just shows up to random things and we chat."

"Okay." Her voice has changed from grateful to very concerned quickly.

"Hannah, do you drink with him often?"

"No." I am frustrated that we are getting far away from the point of my word vomit.

"Okay, there are a few things I am going to ask, and you may be uncomfortable, but I want you to answer them honestly, please. First—what's Raymond's last name, and does he go to your school?"

I am very confused at this point why this would be uncomfortable. "I don't know his last name, and yes."

"Alright...Second, do you think you don't remember because you don't want to?"

Like a ton of bricks, that hits me. A tough one.

"I have misplaced my memory. I can only explain what I can remember and that isn't much. The chalkboard has been wiped mostly clean with only a few spots that I can make out."

I am no longer swinging. I have dead stopped myself, tied myself in a knot, starting to clam up. Scrambling for what should be the correct responses. I'm uncomfortable, but not because I don't want to talk about it. It's because I can't remember anything to bring this situation to light.

"It's not helpful when you keep things from me but even danger-ous when you keep them from yourself. I have a feeling this memory issue you are having is a secret you are keeping. This makes me very nervous, Hannah."

"I don't remember!" I snap, and I am surprised at myself that I am almost yelling. I don't think I have ever done that in this office.

"Okay, Hannah. I am not upset. Please know I am just trying to help you remember so we can clarify." Her voice still an even keel and brings me to a calmer place, but only for a moment until she asks, "My third and last question before we move on is where did that necklace come from?"

Completely taken off guard, puzzled. I look down at my chest, I have Rebecca's necklace that I found in the woods.

I don't know what made me think she wouldn't notice. I have completely changed my outfit today, oddly that's the only thing she has picked out to ask about. Does she already know the answer? Do I just spit it out? I found Rebecca's necklace, and I decided to wear it today and dress in her fashion style.

"I bought it. Rebecca had one, and I admire it."

She definitely doesn't believe me. The look on her face says it all. She knows I am lying about it. Will she call me out?

"We started off doing really well. I don't think you are being truthful with me now."

Damn. How does she catch it every time? I can lie to my mom without issue, but Dr. Psych catches it so instantaneously it's impressive. I suppose it is her job to get into my head and know when I am being deceitful.

"You're right. I didn't want to sound out of my mind. I found it. I went back into the woods behind the barn with Raymond and

I found it by a tree. When I got dressed this morning, I put it on because I didn't want to lose it."

"Now I think you're being mostly truthful. This Raymond came back in a moment of distress to you?"

"Yes, I guess he did." I didn't give it any thought until now. Raymond always seems to be around when I am in some kind of need. Anger, stress, fear—even when I am very sad.

"Does Raymond hang out with anyone else in school? Does he have a group of friends or spend time with a specific group?

"I don't really pay attention to him at school, he hangs out at the wood shop in the basement a lot. Now that I think about it I don't really see him much at all."

"Interesting..." Dr. Psych generally has full attention on me. In this session, it's different. She has a pad of paper she has been writing in with questions, along with my responses to them. Why does today feel so different than normal? She didn't ask about my journal today when I walked in. Come to think of it, she has been really focused on Saturday and not much more.

"Hannah, I don't know if today has been helpful for you, but I am impressed that you have been very open and honest, even in your moments of wandering thought where I see your discomfort. I am going to ask some questions to the district about Raymond, and I think it only fair to be transparent with you about that. It is my understanding the police have found some new information in the case and would like to ask you some questions. I can be there if and when this occurs if you would like. However, I don't have to be. This is a choice you can make now or in the questioning. I will be ready for the rest of the week if they need to call me in. I have explained your treatment and our sessions here in a very general way, but they are aware."

There is no stopping the panic attack from coming on this time. My palms instantly sweaty, my ears and cheeks are on fire. I am struggling to breathe. The cops—what could they possibly want from me? Dr. Psych rushes to her desk and grabs a paper bag. She hands it to me. I shove it to my mouth and breathe in and out, fast at first, and as it's starting to slow, she places her hands on my shoulders and gives me a little squeeze.

"Hannah, the secrets you're keeping from yourself are going to hurt you, not help you. Before you leave this office, are you sure you can't remember anything from this past weekend? I want to help you through this but I can only go as far as you let me in."

We sit quietly for only a moment while I catch my breath. I close my eyes and pull the file in my mind from Saturday night, trying with every bit of strength in me to relive the moments that led to me waking up in that horrible dream. I am physically pushing so hard, I feel a brain aneurysm in my near future.

This isn't working.

It goes blank. Blank sheets of paper for the rest of the story, everything in my mind cleared out. The filing cabinet where my thoughts are kept dumped into recycling and cleared for good.

What is happening to me?

CHAPTER 12

Present

"Hey mom, listen. I have to tell you some things because I feel like some of our issues have been my fault, and I want to tell you what I know of the truth so you can understand some of what's going on inside my head." I know it's not possible for her to actually know what's going on up there, but if I am talking to the police today, I want to at the very least be honest.

I am in deep shit after this conversation though.

"Alright. I am ears wide open." Her mouth almost forms into a grin, like she has been dying for this moment to come along. She won't be smiling in a few minutes, but it's nice to see this is making her happy.

"Okay, so a few months ago, you caught me sneaking back into the house. I know you knew then I was lying about taking pictures late at night, but this is a good place to start. I was at my first party that night. I wasn't drinking, but I was there." The weight on my shoulders physically lifts some.

"I never suspected you were drinking; I knew you were lying to me, which is why your punishment was so long. I thought after a while you would come forward. But you didn't." Sounding disappointed, but still has a visible grin.

"I was drinking this weekend at the party that I also snuck out for. I don't know how much, and I don't know what I was drinking. I have very little memory of that night and the Sunday after. I was in the woods, and I think Rebecca turned around to ask me what I was doing there with her, but I'm not sure if that was real or part of my dream. When you woke me up on Monday morning, I dreamed about being buried alive in those woods and you brought me out of it."

"I am disappointed that you were drinking, although I am not angry with you, I knew that at some point you would get to a point where you would try it. The sneaking out is a whole different conversation that we will be having, but not now. Can I help with remembering anything?"

Taken back by the fact that she is not screaming at me and she is willing to help, I say, "Maybe we can talk about what happened Sunday while I was home and that may jog my memory from the night before. Or even coming home." Surprised I am contracting her into helping me.

"We can do that. Why don't we start tonight with dinner? I'll make something and we can chat about the weekend, see if we can come up with something together. We can talk about sneaking out. I am not going to punish you; I am glad you felt you could tell me." She seems pleased beyond belief. She continues."I know that we have been rocky since the divorce to say the least. I do love you, and I do want the best for you. I think we can both try a little bit harder to work on our relationship in baby steps. Can you tell me why you feel like you need to be open with me now?"

I physically feel my jaw hang open; she wants to build on this.

Why did I think she didn't care at all?

Was that all in my head?

"I love you too, mom. Before I get into the school stuff, do you know what the police want to ask me about?" I wonder if she has seen any more of the case since earlier this week when she had that file.

"I don't know what they are going to ask you. I do know that they were told you were at the party. I don't know who told them or anything other information."

Oh my god, she already knew. No wonder she is so calm. She knew I was there, and she knew I was drinking. She was just holding it like a best kept secret until I revealed myself. I want to be so angry with her right now, but we just took such a leap forward, I hate to back track. I hide my surprise at this conclusion I have come to and reply.

"Okay. I am sure it's not much. I had just thought maybe you knew something, maybe from your office or something..."

We arrived at the school, and I haven't quite divulged everything that I want to, but this was a good start to open a dialog for when we get home later today. She didn't get upset with me. That wasn't a huge secret, but it was enough.

"Thanks for listening. I will see you after school." I close the car door and turn to walk towards the school.

The zoo for the most part has left for the next story. A few locals remain and continue to cover the school with no news to add. There are double the cop cars in the bus loop today that there have been most of this week. I march my way up the steps and through the doors. Peeping in the main office as I walk by, the sheriff catches my eyes and we lock contact. I quickly jolt my eyes back to the ground and walk as quickly as I can without drawing attention. At my locker, I only have to enter the last digit of my combination and push up for it to open. I think everyone does it that way for ease of access. I shove my books in from my bag and grab the one I need for second period. I am late like I am on Mondays because of my visit with the good doctor.

As I slam the locker door, Nate is standing right beside me. I jumped—he scared the daylights out of me.

"I heard you're next, and I am going to be right outside while you're in there. Brendon's dad is the chief. If you don't think I'll find out what you say, you have another thing coming. I have known it was you from the beginning, but no one could prove that you were there. I saw what you threw away, and I brought it right to the cops for them to see what you have been up to. Better be ready, freak." He turns around and heads away from the hall I have to turn down. Thankful for that in this moment.

I know he saw me throw the rag away. What did that have to do with him?

Why is he dead set that I had something to do with this?

I take a quick breath in, shake my head to clear my thoughts and head down the hall away from Nate to my class to steer as clear as possible. I just make it to the door of my classroom and the teacher is standing in the frame. I put my head down trying my hardest to avoid him. Ugly orange pass in hand, he swings his arm to interrupt my entry into the room.

"You are needed in the office today, Hannah. Please go there now." Handing me the pass, my heart drops to my stomach, and I know this is it.

"May I go to the bathroom first?" I can feel the tears welling in my eyes. Any second, one will drop to my cheek.

"Yes, be quick about it and then straight to the office."

Scattering to try and compose my thoughts. I didn't think it would be so fast. I dash down the hallway and turn away from the office instead of towards it, to get to the bathroom first. I swing open the door so hard it hits the wall and echoes throughout the bathroom. Thankfully no one else is in here. I throw my backpack to the floor under one of the sinks and put my hands on either side of the cold porcelain staring into the drain.

Okay, Hannah, this is fine. They know you were there; they are just trying to find Rebecca. Talking to me could help with the investigation. It's going to be okay.

Shooting my eyes from the sink drain to the mirror, I stare at my swollen eyes and examine my hair, which is all over the place as if I just spent the last hour throwing up. I turn the warm water on and put my hands under it. Instantly a warm flush runs through my entire body. I turn off the water and flick my hands to get rid of most of the water, using what's left to pat down my hair.

I wish at this moment that I could remember everything that happened this weekend. I wish that I could be more helpful to the investigation. I want to help find Rebecca. I am saddened for her parents and terrified for her. I had better hurry, the police will think I am hiding something if I take much longer. I give my hair one more quick pat down and run my fingers over my braid, wipe under my eyes and run through the door as fast as I came in. Walking down the hall and taking in my surroundings, it's overly quiet. All the students are in class, and there isn't anyone roaming the halls or chatter.

Arriving at the office door and just about to walk in, out of the corner of my eye, I spy Nate. Skulking through the hallway, stopping at the corner, just enough of him showing to have me right in his line of sight. I gasp in air, abruptly open the office door and shut it behind me. Realizing that everyone in the room now has their eyes on me while I stand there breathing in and out quickly, and my back up against the office door. Like I am running away from something. Now everyone knows it.

I look down at the ground taking in the odd color of the carpet in this room, almost a burnt orange. Principal Martinez is standing in front of me when I snap out of it and look back up.

"Hannah are you alright? What's the matter?" The concern in his voice is comforting. I don't answer him.

"Okay, Hannah. Okay." Principal Martinez smiles. "These nice police officers are going to ask you some questions about this weekend and some of the events. We need you to be honest with them in hopes of finding Rebecca. There will be a woman from child services in the room as well as an attorney to protect your rights and advise you if needed. I have to ask because we are aware of your treatment status—do you want your mom or Dr. Psych present in the room with you?"

"No, I am okay without them." Answering in a very timid manner, moreso than I am usually. I can't recall a time that I have even spoken to Principal Martinez as often as I have this week.

"Alright Hannah, do you understand that any information is helpful, but it is on the record and you are not required to answer anything you don't feel comfortable answering?"

"Yes, I understand." I feel like he might be on my side with this one, calming my mood.

"If you're ready, they are ready for you in the room and we can get this started. You should be able to return to class soon." His tone is so relaxing. I feel better about this already.

"I'm ready."

CHAPTER 13

Present

I thought he said they were ready for me, but Principal Martinez stuck me in his office in this uncomfortable wooden chair waiting, and they have all been outside the door talking amongst themselves for the last ten minutes. Drinking coffee and not even looking in my direction. No sign of Nate anywhere around the area—that's a relief. I suppose it's possible they are waiting for someone; maybe the child advocate isn't here yet, or the attorney. Reassuring that they are truly trying to protect my rights, although with my mom being an attorney herself, they are probably just covering their butts. I wonder why my mom wouldn't have insisted she be here. I guess it's possible she doesn't think it's a very big deal, which maybe it isn't.

The office I am in is completely glass. There is no privacy in this room, and I can see out in every direction. What does the principal need privacy for? I wouldn't know, seems odd to just be in a glass house for eight hours a day. His office is so plain—a few pictures of his family on his desk, a cup of half drank coffee on a coaster in front of his laptop. A filing cabinet in the far corner on the only actual half of a wall he has, picture frames with his diplomas hung above.

I keep moving my hands in an attempt not to bite my fingernails because I am so anxious. The waiting is not helping that in the least. I have taken apart my braid and put it back together a minimum of four times while waiting for whatever it is I am waiting for. Just as I am about to give up on my mission to not bite my nails, the sheriff with an entourage comes through the door. No longer smiling and laughing, now all straight faced and silent.

Is this to intimidate or to heed a warning?

"Hello, Hannah. I am Sheriff Lybecker. This is Mrs. Cooper from Child Services and Mrs. Leigh with the minor assigned attorney's office. They are going to be here in case you have any questions, and they will suggest to you which questions if any not to answer. You will meet with them again after the interview to continue your conversation. Do you understand all of this so far?" He's very direct, but friendly enough that I feel comfortable answering questions for him.

I am eyeing the Child Services lady up and down—a medium height, stocky build, African American woman with tight woven braids pulled back into a neat bun. Deep brown eyes and pouty pink lips, all natural in comparison to her counterpart, the minor assigned attorney.

"Yes, I understand." My voice is buried into my chest as I am looking down to avoid eye contact while I answer.

"Hannah, I am going to need you to speak clearly and towards us because I have to record this conversation. Do you understand and agree to this?" He looks to Mrs. Cooper for approval for what he has just asked me. She looks me in the eyes and nods in my direction as if to say this is protocol and this is okay.

I pull my head up, take a deep breath and clearly reply with, "Yes."

"Good, good. Alright, is everyone in this room ready to proceed?"

All in unison, they say, "Yes."

My chair is facing the rest of the office where everyone else is facing me so they can't see who just walked in. Nate... he is standing just beyond the glass with Brendon talking to his dad, the chief of police. I can not catch my breath fast enough at this moment. I know that he is going to be here for the duration of this meeting if he's able.

"This is a recording in the case of Rebecca Jones, missing person, interview with Hannah Flynn to commence on Thursday the 10th day of May." Speaking to the recorder, very matter of fact. "We start this interview with me asking you to state your name and age for the record please."

"Hannah Flynn. I am seventeen years old." I reply

"Great, Hannah, thank you. Can you tell me where you were Saturday night, the 5th day of May?" He breathes heavy, seeming to regret my response before I say it.

Mrs. Cooper, the child advocate, looks at me and nods her head in approval to answer, and then leans over to my ear and whispers.

"Answer the question without going into detail for now—just where you were that night." Her tone is sweet, and she smells of flowery perfume that tickles my nose but I think I enjoy it.

"I was at a party with a group of people at the old abandoned farmhouse near the woods." I am quiet but clear with my answer, and I start to fidget with my fingernails.

"Okay, Hannah. I appreciate the honesty given the situation at hand. Did you see Rebecca Jones at this party?"

"Yes." As directed, I don't go into detail, just answer the question. Out of the corner of my eye, I see that Nate has moved from right in front of me in the office to the right-hand side of the office where I can only see the tip of his nose and his hair.

Why is he still lingering in the office? Is he really watching me while I am questioned?

Mrs. Cooper and Mrs. Leigh leaned into one another, whispering. Mrs. Leigh looked in my direction and nodded her head.

Mrs. Cooper leans back to me and whispers, "If you are uncomfortable here, we can stop for now and go to the station, or I can have them meet in your home. All you have to do is say the word."

"No, I am okay," I whisper in return. I stop fidgeting with my nails because I assume that's what tipped her off to thinking I can't make it through this. I can still see Nate standing on the right side of the office. I can no longer see Brendon, so my assumption is that he has left and no longer wishes to watch the "freak show".

"Hannah, did you see Rebecca leave the party into the woods?"

My blood starts to pump harder, and my heart beat picks up. "Yes."

"Do you know where she went from there? Did she go with her friends somewhere in the woods? Did she drive off in a car maybe? Did she leave with Nate?"

I am twiddling my thumbs together during all of these questions. A flash comes across my eyes— blonde hair swinging around. Her eyes meet mine; she looks me up and down.

"What are you doing here?" I ask.

Mrs. Cooper reaches up and puts her hand on my shoulder. "Hannah, I know this is a lot, but anything you remember will help just try to think back."

"I don't remember anything like that."

Nate has moved from behind the one wall in the office to where I can see his whole face now. He laughs, glances up and stabs me in the face with his glare.

"Okay, Hannah, you're doing great. I have a few more questions, and we will be done for now. Try to remember that night as clearly as you can. Did you go with anyone?"

"No." This was true. I didn't go with anyone; I technically went alone.

"Another student saw you there going into the woods shortly after Rebecca. Did you go into the woods that night?"

"Yes, but..."

Mrs. Leigh stands and puts her hand on my knee, moving softly as if to tell me "not now, Hannah". I swallow hard and nod to her as if I understand.

"Yes." The words leave my lips in a squeak trying to hold myself back. I look beyond the room, and Nate has found his way back around to the front of the office in conversation. His back is to me, with his arms crossed and leaning against the glass.

"A student also witnessed that when you arrived at school late on Monday, you had thrown away a red rag with some screws wrapped inside in a classroom garbage can. Can you tell me about that?"

Swallowing the lump in my throat and forcing words to come from my mouth. "No."

"We found some chemicals on that rag. I don't suppose you know how that got there do you?"

"No." No one else is in the office beyond this room now except Nate. He is facing the room and peering in. I am not sure if he can hear us or if he is just watching our facial expressions.

"Alright, Hannah, one more quick question, and I will leave you to talk to these fine ladies until we can revisit this. Do you have the clothes you were wearing the night of the party at your home?"

"Yes." I reach up to put my hand around my neck and realize I am still wearing Rebecca's necklace. I haven't taken it off. What if they have noticed? What am I going to say? The door flies open, slamming against the glass, and it shatters on impact. I have always thought how unsafe it is to be in a room where the door can cause the glass to break so easily.

As he flies through the room so forcefully, he scares me, and I stand up. Everyone in the room has their jaws hanging on the floor, in awe of what is happening. Nate grabs the chair that I was sitting on and, like a rubber ball, picks it up by the armrest and tosses it aside. He grabs a hold of my neck with one hand and is squeezing so tight I can't get any words out. He slams me onto the ground, my head just missing the desk as I go down. I can barely breathe. The air isn't coming into my mouth to gain access to my lungs. I am terrified I am going to die. He picks my head off the ground and slams it back down; with his free hand he grasps the necklace around my neck. Plucks it off, as easily as a toothpick, it breaks the chain.

Holding it in his fist, he screams, "Where did you get this? Why are you wearing it? You think this is funny? I'm about to show you funny, freak!"

I have no strength to get words out. My lips and tongue are dry. The grasp Nate has around my neck has not given way even a little. There is a glaze coming over my eyes, so I can barely make out his face anymore. Within seconds, I can't see him at all, and the room is completely black.

The last bit I hear is, "Get him off her! Get him in restraints."
From a different side of the room, "We need an ambulance, stat!"

CHAPTER 14

Eight Years Ago

"Hannah, why don't you and Alyssa go play outside? I'll get the grill going and we will have some lunch in a few."

"Okay, mom. We will be over by the tree house."

"That's fine, Hannah. Stay away from the pool. Your dad hasn't put the gate up around it yet."

"I know, mom, I know." I turned to my friend. "Come on. Let's go play princesses, and we can be locked in the tower."

Giggly little girls playing dress up in a treehouse built just for me in one of the tallest trees I have ever seen in my life. Alyssa always has two french braids tied into pigtails in her silky copper-tone hair. Today, she just has two separate complete french braids on either side of her head. I get a little jealous. because her hair is so straight and mine is so curly. I can't have french braids or pigtails. It's too puffy, and doesn't look like hers, or even close. There is a lady down the street that can tame my hair. She tries to get me in once a week, and shows my mom how to help. Alyssa and I both have the same color eyes though. We could be twins if her hair was curly like mine. Or mine straight like hers.

Alyssa and I have been friends for a while now. She moved in down the street about a year ago, and one day we were walking and ran into her family. My mom and dad invited them over for a cookout, and instantly we were great friends. She's two years older than me, but we have a lot in common. She likes to read, write, and play pretend. She doesn't like to swim and I do, but she never learned how and they don't have a pool at their house. She also plays piano, which she is trying to teach me to do too. She just started looking at makeup and boys, which I have no interest in, but I follow along with her interest because that's what good friends do. My mom and dad really like her parents. They get along really well. They have cookouts and drinks often; it has become a weekend ritual around here.

The end of the summer is coming and we will be in different schools next year. It's sad to think about. I have been in this neighborhood since I started school, and I don't have any other real friends like Alyssa. My mom is starting the grill and getting on the phone to call over Alyssa's parents for lunch. We head up to the treehouse to start playing. I think everything is a typical day. Alyssa just got back from her grandparents' house a few hours away, so I am so excited to hear everything she did there.

We reach the top of the treehouse and close the door to the floor. She has a purse today that I must not have noticed she had when she got to my house. As she closes the door, she says "Okay, kid, let's do your hair and your makeup." She dumps the contents of her purse on the floor, and everything in there to do a makeover.

"*Kid*?" I snort in reply. Our age difference has never felt so far away from each other.

"I thought we were going to dress up and play princesses hiding from the dragon below." The dragon happens to be my dad on a lawn mower, but who's for the details?

"What better way to play princess than to look like one?" She lifts one eyebrow.

"How was your grandma's house this year?" I start to make light conversation. She rips through my hair with a brush.

"Your hair is so soft but so tangled. What do you use to get through it?"

Annoyed that she ignored my question, I say, "I don't know. My mom puts some oil in it and it lets the brush go through."

She sifts through the items on the floor, searching for something to help brush through my curly mess.

"Oh, this should work then," pulling out some leave-in conditioning spray.

"So, did you learn some new songs on the piano at your grandma's?" Trying to take the focus off my hair.

"No, I didn't use the piano this time. I met some new friends that taught me a few ways to do my makeup and I have been obsessed ever since. They did a full makeover on me, and I couldn't wait to come home and do yours."

I gleam at the thought that she was thinking of me while she was away, even while making new friends. She keeps pulling through my hair, although the spray did help—it stopped the pain of her pulling and now the brush runs through mostly smooth. My dad hooked up power up here, so we have lights and outlets and even a light up mirror, thinking that I was going to be into makeup and boys soon also. Alyssa has a black tool plugged into the outlet. It must be getting hot because it's steaming and just let out an irritating beep. She pulls out a little comb to part my hair, and takes the rest of my hair and clips it out of the way.

"We are going to straighten your hair today. Have you ever done that?"

I am almost terrified to respond not knowing if this is going to hurt, and shake my head "no" in response to her.

"Perfect. You're going to love it. Your hair is going to look like mine, only better, because it will be down with a little wave."

I gulp. "Okay."

"Don't worry, this doesn't hurt. Just don't pull away from me really fast or lean your head into me so I don't burn you or pull your hair out."

I nod, and she starts in at the first layer of hair.

"You know, next year I'll be in a different school, but you can have this straightener if you want to be able to look like this while you're in school. We can go shopping and pick you up some make up if you like how I do it too. It will be fun!" I can't for the life of me explain her excitement. This is not what I had planned for today.

It seems like hours, and finally, she has finished with my hair. It feels so strange on my shoulders— it's heavier than normal and seems so much longer. My hair is straight almost to my butt in the back. It does feel somewhat cooler to have straight hair. My head usually sweats during the summer heat. My mom calls up and says lunch is ready and her parents must also be here because I hear them call for Alyssa.

Alyssa opens the door to the treehouse and says, "We have a surprise for you guys. We will be down in a few minutes once it's finished." She turns back to face me and says, "Okay, now let's wipe your face and get some makeup on there. Nothing big, just a touch to bring out those pretty eyes."

I am starting to see why people go to spas. This is pretty relaxing, and I like having someone touch my hair other than my mom. Most people don't offer to do my hair because it's so curly. I think it scares them. I think that she is handing me a wipe to wash my face with, and I put my hands out to grab it.

She smacks my hands and says, "Nope, pretend you're having a face massage. I am going to do it all."

I am actually pretty upset that she had the audacity to smack my hand out of the way like a child reaching for cookies before having dinner. I try to fake a smile and hide my complete repulsion for my friend Alyssa at this moment.

"Okay, I will try and relax." I drop my smile and close my eyes.

She wipes down my face and grabs some product from the floor, squirts it into her hands and then rubs it all over. She explains that it's some moisturizer, which in my mind is lotion, which seems like a disaster on my sweaty skin. Next, she pulls out some creamy stuff that looks like face coloring crayon in a bottle. She puts it on a brush and rubs it all over my face. Then with a different brush, she puts some powder that looks like baby powder—but less white—on.

"We are almost done! I can't wait for you to see how even your face looks right now. And the freckles all over your face are completely hidden."

Am I supposed to hide my freckles? I am not really sure what that was supposed to mean.

With a tiny doll brush, she has me close my eyes and puts some color on my eyelids. I open my eyes multiple times during this process, which causes her to giggle at me. She has this black stick in her hand that must really be a colored pencil, looks at my face and says, "We will skip the eye, it will look bad with your complexion. We don't want you to be gothic right?"

"What's gothic?"

She giggles again at my response and says, When you get to middle school, you'll understand. Okay, now mascara is really simple. All you do is blink when I say blink, and we will be all done. I hope you like it. You look so pretty."

"Blink," Alyssa says.

"Okay, and blink."

"Blink."

"One more time."

"Repeat on the other eye."

I can't believe that women get up extra early just to do all this. I would have to get up at like three in the morning just to accomplish all of this—especially my hair. It seems like so much wasted time, and on what?

"You. Look. Radiant! Eeek!"

My eyes widen right up with her screech of joy.

She hands me a mirror and says, "Well what do you think?"

I actually kind of like it. I look like a whole different person. "I like it."

"Oh, good! I am so glad. You look fabulous! I know you don't wash your hair everyday with how curly it is, so as long as you keep it out of water, it should stay straight until you have to wash it again. You can keep this though. I have a couple at home."

Wow, that's really it. No pretending, no dragons, no princess, no castle. What has changed in such a short time? Why don't I understand this difference in Alyssa, and why do I feel so left behind? She packs all her belongings back into the oversized purse she brought up with her, and opens the floor door to walk down. We leave the treehouse and walk towards the house. My dad is lounging in a chair, and my mom has just finished cooking. Alyssa's parents are laughing and talking about random adult happenings and the weekly gossip in the neighborhood.

My dad looks up and pushes his glasses down. "Oh, Hannah, sweet pea! You look beautiful."

"Thanks, dad!" That makes it so much better.

"Oh my, Hannah. That's very different, but I like it," my mom replies. She has been obsessed with my curly hair forever, so I know she isn't actually very happy.

Alyssa's mom and dad look up at me as well. "Hannah, darling, you look so good. Alyssa, did you do that for her?" Alyssa nods her head to her mother's question. "Isn't that so sweet of you!"

We all sit down and enjoy some lunch, talking about the end of the summer and the fond memories we have made. Wishing that we had much more time to enjoy the weather, the days off and each other's company. My mom and dad start to pack up the food from the table. My dad comes out of the house with a few beers for him and Alyssa's dad. They must be staying for a while longer. I haven't been able to stop running my fingers through my hair. It feels so nice. I can't usually do it like this.

"Mom, can we just sit by the pool since you guys are all here? Just with our feet in?"

"Yes, honey, if you want to go in you can now, but sitting by the side is fine too."

We take off our flip flops and dip our feet into the pool, trying to enjoy every last laugh the summer has to offer. We sat there for an hour giggling like toddlers, and talking about all the things we encountered over the summer. Now that my makeup is done and she got it out of her system, Alyssa tells me about her grandparents' house and her new friends she made while she was there.

The sun is starting to set, and they are getting ready to pack up the evening to leave. It is Sunday so they all have to work in the morning, even if we don't have school just yet.

Alyssa turns to me and speaks. "It's been really great being your friend, and I hope when you get to middle school in a couple years we can be just as close. I don't think we will see each other much once school starts, so maybe we should leave our friendship off on a good note."

My jaw literally drops. We just had such a great day; she has introduced me to all these new things, talking about how great we have been together. And now she wants to end our friendship? I don't get it.

"So, we aren't friends anymore? I can feel tears forming, so I swallow to hold them back because that will just make this so much worse.

"I just think with you being younger, and I won't see you in school for a while we are going to part ways anyhow, so why not end it in a spot where we are both in a great place and genuinely happy?"

At this very moment, I have no idea how it happens but as the words leave her mouth, she's in the pool. She is screaming for me to help her and tossing up and down, taking on water. Our parents are in the house.

"Hannah!"

"Hannah, please!"

"Hannah!"

Her voice is desperate, raspy and clutching for air, in between gargles. I just sit there. Watching her struggle, not moving. She sinks to the bottom of the pool, and next to me her dad comes through like superman. Jumps into the water, grabs a hold of Alyssa and resurfaces. He throws her up on the poolside and jumps over the edge. He starts to pump on her chest and breathes into her mouth, the whole time saying, "Come on kiddo, breathe! Come on, kid, you're still in there. You've got to breathe."

She slings forward and coughs up a ton of water, sitting up and spewing all the water from in her lungs. She is crying so very hard. She looks in my direction.

"What the hell was that, Hannah? You were just going to let me drown because I am too old for baby games? Stay away from me forever, you freak of nature! And give me my stuff back!" she shouts.

"Wait, kiddo, calm down. Let's talk about this. Maybe you just slipped getting up and it seemed like you were pushed because it was so sudden?" Her dad is trying to calm her down and convince her that I couldn't have tried to harm her.

"No, dad, she shoved me right off the side because I told her we should part ways in our friendship, that I was getting older." Alyssa stands to her feet, stomps over to the table where I put the straightener. She snatches it up and looks right at me. "Don't come near me ever again. We aren't friends or acquaintances, and definitely not doing anything together ever again."

My parents are now standing in the doorway listening to the whole thing, and the look of worry on both of their faces is palpable. I actually can't grasp that I just did that.

Did I mean to do that?

I wasn't trying to drown her. Was I?

I know she can't swim, but would my feelings being hurt cause me to end her life?

I try to wrap my head around the events that have just taken place. I haven't said anything to anyone yet. I stare at the ground and recall the moments leading up to the supposed push off the edge. She said that we should end our friendship now while we are in a great place. The rage that came over my body was like someone else took over. It was almost like little worms climbed into my head, took control of my brain and did whatever it was they needed to do to make me back to normal. I could feel how red my cheeks were from the heat. I could feel it radiating off of them. My head was sweating, even in my perfectly straight hair look. My palms clammy, the tension in my face causing me to clench my jaw as hard as I could bare. Next thing I knew, the rage was so strong I slapped both my hands on Alyssa's back and shoved her right into the pool.

Even knowing she can't swim. I don't care. How could she do that to me?

I really did do that...

"I'm sorry. I panicked and didn't know how to get you out or what I was going to do. I was upset and I didn't mean to hurt you," I yell at her as she is storming through the glass door into the house to leave.

I received no answer in return from her.

That was the last time I ever saw or spent time with Alyssa.

CHAPTER 15

Eight Years Ago

Shortly after the event, Alyssa's parents stop coming over all together. When they were still coming over, they refused to be in the backyard with us. We had to sit inside or in the front yard. Alyssa never came back with them. All they said about it was "too many memories" and shook it off. We started school, and I thought I might see her on the bus and maybe we could chat, and at least still end on a good note. She has her dad drive her to school every day, she never rides the bus. We don't pass each other in the hall, or even see each other at the library or in pep rallies or school assemblies. Honestly, I could have transferred schools, and I wouldn't even know the difference.

Within a few months of the following school year, my parents stopped being invited to the block parties and gatherings.

They were told they couldn't risk me being around their kids. Which isn't fair—my parents had nothing to do with it. It isn't their fault I couldn't control my anger.

I started to see a counselor at school because I had slipped into a state of depression. At my age, it's bewildering to my parents that I would have anything to be that upset about. They don't realize the feeling of loss for Alyssa that left a gaping hole inside me. And I could see what was happening to them because of me. They were losing their sense of home in the spot we have been since I was born. The house became toxic, and my parents didn't do anything but fight and scream. Kept me up half the night from their constant banter back and forth. I know they tried not to, but they were unhappy, and really, how could they not be? They had the perfect life before I tried to drown the neighborhood sweetheart.

I could see the end was near, and things were going to take a big change in all of our lives. I started to see a psychologist named Dr. Psych. It had been two years since the incident with Alyssa, and nothing had gotten better. My rage was becoming increasingly worse. I was having trouble in school. I couldn't keep any friends and I kept having lost moments of thought. My parents tried their best, and who could blame them? The doctor put me on meds to stabilize myself. Which worked when I took them, but when I didn't, I would lose hours of my life doing God knows what. It wasn't long before I was so out of tone that they started to have sit down conversations about getting divorced. I hadn't realized yet that dad was struggling with the same things I was. I could blame it on being too young to notice but really, I was too focused on myself. We moved to a new house, new school district, new neighborhood in hopes of refreshing, and shortly after we got there, everything was settling in. Dad moved out. He went far away at first, to a place we couldn't visit, and then he moved kind of close. I couldn't visit him as often as I wanted but my mom made a point once a week to make sure I was able to visit.

Little did I know then, the move, the divorce, dad's relocation, had nothing to do with me or my friend Alyssa. Not even the incident or what I was going through. Down the road aways, I finally asked my mom, and when things were still in a good spot, she actually told me what had happened to them. I might as well have been a ghost during this time.

About Three Years Ago

Sitting at the table eating leftovers from the night before, and my mom actually doesn't have work glued to her face.

"Mom, did Dad leave because of what happened with Alyssa at the old house?"

She drops the noodles off her fork and stares blankly back at me. "No, honey. Why in the world would you ever think that?"

I shrug my shoulders. "Well, we moved shortly after that. You stopped being invited to parties because of me, the neighbors stopped coming over and it was like I ruined your whole life, including your marriage."

Shocked at my response, she pats the napkin to her mouth and puts both hands on the table as if to brace herself for what's coming. "Oh Hannah! No, you had nothing to do with anything that happened between the move, the divorce, dad's new confines or anything like that."

My jaw physically drops in complete shock at the newfound information.

None of it was my fault at all. Is that even really possible?

"Oh my gosh, Hannah. No, why wouldn't you have asked me about this sooner? I think you're able to handle what really happened if you would like me to share?" She moves and touches my hand so softly to offer her embrace, like I am going to jump out of my chair and sit on her lap.

I pull my hand from hers and look at it expecting to find a burn mark or something—I am not sure. I turn my eyes back to her intently. "Yes, if you're willing to share, I would really like to know. All this time I thought it was my fault. All of it."

My mom rubs her hands together, then intertwines her fingers and rests them back on the table. "Okay, Hannah. The night that you pushed Alyssa into the water"

"She fell." I cut her off

"We have talked about this, and you have admitted at points that you may have helped her fall knowing that she couldn't swim." Her brows furrow, and she raises her eyes to meet my face.

"Alright." I agree, even if I don't truly believe it.

"Can I go on?" She asks, annoyed, but I am glad that she is still willing to finish talking to me. I nod my head once to her, signaling to continue, and that I will no longer interrupt her.

"So, the night that happened, you weren't aware that your dad and the neighbor were arguing already that evening about something unrelated. Shortly after the incident, the arguments between them became more and more intense. During one of the neighborhood parties a few weeks after the incident—which you weren't there for only because you were at your grandmother's that evening. Not because you were not invited or everyone had shunned you from the surrounding areas. The neighbor approached your father and I, and said that your dad was sleeping with his wife. Which caught everyone there off guard, because of course they thought that we were both perfect couples in the neighborhood." She snarks at her own remark. She shifts in her seat, looking to be uncomfortable.

"I had no way to prove whether that was true or not, but I stood by your dad's side and put myself in the middle and argued "there is no way that is possible; you must be mistaken". The neighbors' reply to me was that your dad and I were just as delusional just like our daughter, and no wonder she is a Looney Toon. Now, Hannah, I don't think we have ever talked about the fact that your dad is on the same medicine you are on for various reasons that he and I have dealt with throughout the years."

I gasp. I knew he was in a facility, but now it is starting to make more sense that he is in a mental institution of some kind. She continues while nodding her head to reassure the information I am trying to absorb so quickly is true.

"It never really got out of control until after that party. Your dad was so upset about the remark about you and his infidelity that he waited until I was asleep and snuck out. He went over to the neighbor's house and…" Tears well up into her eyes. She has her hands cuffed to her face, unsure if she wants to tell me the rest.

"Hannah, your dad is a great person, and I want you to know that he stopped taking his medicine for a few days before this happened. He is unwell and needs the medicine to be stable. To my knowledge, this was the first time anything like this ever happened." She takes the deepest breath in, holds it for a few seconds and releases. Looks around the room, back at me, and powers through.

"Hannah, your dad killed the neighbor. Alyssa's father."

My eyes are as wide as I can hold them open. I fix my mouth to respond. "How?"

Shocked, that is the question that I ask. I wonder now if she is still willing to share so much information with me.

She hesitates. "Maybe we should finish this conversation with Dr. Psych involved?"

I snapped quickly, "No, I want to know!"

"Okay, okay, but we have to talk about this together on her next visit, okay?"

"Alright, mom, I promise." Losing patience and hanging on the edge of my seat now.

"He stabbed him a few times with a kitchen knife from the house. He didn't try to run or hide what he had done. He knew that it was wrong, but he couldn't keep himself in check. I know you know what that feels like, and that's why I try so hard to protect you the best that I can. Since he is unstable, they didn't lock him away in a jail cell and throw away the key. They allowed him in mental facilities and as he becomes more stable, he is able to move to different spots and have more privileges. Unfortunately, he will be there for a while, and after that he may have to be in a different style home, but that will be up to the court." Her shoulders visibly lighter—that must have been some weight.

"That's why we had to move? And the divorce?" I have so many more questions, but if I shoot them rapid fire, she will clam up and stop talking or decide that is enough for now.

"Yes, I stayed with your dad through court, but we filed for the divorce somewhere in the middle, mostly to keep you protected from the accusations and hearsay that was going around. If we were divorced, they couldn't question you about his character. We acted like we had been separated for a while."

"So, the arguments that you had didn't have anything to do with me? It was all this going on in the background." I am almost relieved that this was all about something totally unrelated to Alyssa. I am a little dumbfounded that I didn't realize dad was in a mental hospital. I wonder if the affair really happened, but I don't dare ask.

"Yes Hannah, everything that was going had nothing to do with you and Alyssa. When you didn't see Alyssa in school, it was because her mom had her moved to a private school. The fighting, the parties, all the gossip in the neighborhood had nothing to do with you. It was all talk about what your dad did. I really don't think he was having an affair. I never got a chance to hear why he thought that your dad was sleeping with his wife, and I may never know the answer to that question, but I truly believe he wouldn't have done that."

Wow. I didn't expect her to disclose that so freely. I feel better that she did though. She even said that my dad is a great guy. That took me back for sure. Both our dinners untouched while we were talking, my mom moves from the table, grabs my plate and puts it in the microwave to heat it up for me. We stay silent for the next few minutes, unsure how to recoup from such a serious conversation. She grabs my plate from the microwave, sets it in front of me and says "Finish up so we can get ready for bed."

CHAPTER 16 - THE CAPTAIN

<u>Present</u>

I have been a captain on this force now for twenty years, and in all my years, I have yet to encounter these circumstances. One of the top families in the community is missing a child going on almost a week now. The percentage of people being dead after going missing grows with each day that passes. If it wasn't for the family and who they are, we would have already had the conversation about the likelihood that we are looking for a body and not a person. Rebecca's family has lived here almost her whole life. Her old man hit rich a while back from buying some really lucky stocks at the perfect time. Picture-perfect family they are, and not the snooty nose-in-the-air type of rich either. Always giving back. Rebecca is not the type of girl to just run off. We have had a few cases where knowing the kids at the school has been helpful. A few cases of run-offs, I was able to wait it out, and they eventually came home or were located.

This isn't the same.

Rebecca is a sweet girl, always involved in all of the community activities. Head cheerleader, lead role in the high school play, a real go-getter. I have even seen her make cookies for the elderly home around the corner from the library for no special reason, just because. Last year, one of the students was sick, had leukemia, and Rebecca held a fundraiser for her. Sent her to Disney World so she could see Mickey Mouse before she met her unfortunate end. All those treatments really were hard on her poor little body. Rebecca was there at the hospital for her until the day she died. Then held a celebration at her home for the memory of the girl. Raised enough money for the foundation and the family to help them move. Pretty sure she is still in contact with them. I have run into them from time to time around here, assuming that they are staying in Rebecca's family home. Caring people like that don't just disappear off the face of the earth overnight. The signs would have been pretty clear. And if she was planning on running, she definitely wouldn't run away without Nate.

Those two remind me of my lovely wife and myself. When I first started on the force so many years ago down in Texas, we were inseparable just like those two. Although when we first started this search, I thought for sure that boy had something to do with it. The way he was acting was just completely erratic, uncontrollable.

He was the only one that the partygoers could remember actually going into the woods to find her. No one had an exact timeline, but they all thought he was gone for a while, and next they knew, he appeared, got in his truck and took off. Didn't speak a word to anyone, not even to let them know that Rebecca was gone. That must have cleared the party—everyone scared out of their wits trying to figure out what had Nate so spooked to just leave. He still hasn't revealed what led him onto what he saw or heard to know that she was missing. Nate went to Rebecca's residence to find her parents. We all flew out to make a report instantly and went on our search.

The fire was still going, but not a single soul remained. I am sure they were drinking and didn't want to get busted. Once they realized how severe the situation was, they all came forward with their accounts from that evening. The text line amongst teenagers is stronger and faster than any newscasting I have seen in this lifetime. All with similar stories, all with minimal memory, confirming our suspicion of alcohol being involved in the party. No real leads to work with and no eye witness of her leaving the party or even her disappearance—just there one minute, and then into the woods without a trace.

Nate is so sure and has been since the minute that Rebecca went missing that Hannah had something to do with her disappearance. Hannah has never been involved in much. She's pretty intelligent from what I can gather, but not in Rebecca's circle.

Hannah's current situation, we will have to wait for her to receive some treatment and wait for Dr. Psych's approval to question her once again. Once we have some evidence to present, we will have a better idea what questions we will need to address with her. I can't imagine that Hannah had anything to do with Rebecca disappearing, but realistically, it's the only true lead we have at this current moment. Nate bruised her up pretty good. He should have never been close enough to the principal's office to witness her questioning. I guess sometimes I forget that I look the other way with some of these kids due to the friendship they have with my son. I know that isn't the most moral thing being the captain. Most of these kids are good kids, and I don't think that Nate meant to lose it quite that way. The kid looked like he hadn't slept in days, though. My guess is he isn't eating very much either. That can be a dangerous combination for anyone, but especially an athlete who has a regime.

We hadn't found anything to prove or disprove that Hannah was there or not there. We hadn't found anything to connect her to Rebecca at all until Nate watched Hannah throw something in the garbage. Now, we are a pretty small town over here, so we don't have a lot of fancy machines to test DNA or chemicals or anything like that. The rag that Nate saw Hannah throw away in class had some screws wrapped in it, with a substance that looked like blood. We had to send that up to the city to have some tests run.

While we waited for the results, I thought we could do one sweep to see if we found anything matching the screws or the rag to the woods. At bare minimum, it might give us some kind of lead.

We have searched every inch of the barn; it did occur to me that there are some tools and screws inside. Might be time for a closer look. Before we left the office, I took some pictures of the screws that Nate brought to us and decided to explore the barn and see if I could find anything that really sticks out. Sliding the large door to the left just enough of an opening for me to fit my body through. The smell is musty, like stale crackers. The light shines through like a beacon attempting to share all of the barn's secrets with me. Can't put my finger on why, but I love the smell inside this old barn. It has been abandoned since before we moved to town. The family that owns the property is long gone from this world to the next. The state acquired the land some years ago and never did anything with it. The dusty floor is flooded with the prints of my crew and I walking in and out in the pursuit of Rebecca.

On one of the walls is a board with hundreds of tiny holes and metal prongs affixed to them to hold the tools. Each tool has a vivid outline from sitting in here for so long exposed to very few elements. Not a single one with rust, but all covered in dust. I examine more closely as I walk towards the board. Two tools from the board have been disrupted. The dust from where they lie now doesn't quite match up. I pull a white latex glove from my pocket, slide it on my hand, snap a quick picture with my phone to notate the position of the ball peen hammer. As I reach to grab the tool from its hook, I look down briefly to see I am stepping on screws all over the ground. I hadn't realized how many there are in this building. They had no relevance in my mind, so I must have just blanked them out.

Before I take a picture and compare the screw to the ones Nate found disposed of, I fix my eyes to the tools once again. Picking up the wood handle of the hammer to examine, I see the smallest speck of red in the top edge of the head. The suspicions of us maybe looking for a body flood so quickly with the thought of this being a possible murder weapon. My worst fear was realized at this very moment.

I don't think there is a way we are going to find Rebecca alive and hiding out. I think we are going to find her already gone, and possibly even from the day she went missing.

The screwdriver that seems to also be out of place on the wall, recently used, doesn't appear to have any blood on it. I snap a picture and take that for my collection as well. Now for the screws on the ground. My gut has already let me know that these are the same as the ones found with the rag Hannah threw away. I am struggling with the thought that this is possible. Hannah may have really had something to do with the disappearance of Rebecca. I snap pictures, throw everything into bags and walk out the doors to meet some of my team to fill them in on what I have just found.

The barn wasn't the only place we have searched multiple times but also the field, the corn and the forest. The whole force has had every single shift available for days, waiting for some ounce of a clue where Rebecca may be, or even worse—where her body may be. The forest is so dense that even in the daytime, it's hard to see without a flashlight. With one, you can't see too far in front of your face anyways. I keep the hope alive, telling myself we are going to come up with some clue, some evidence that leads us in the right direction. I could still be wrong, and she is hiding out somewhere after an argument with her parents or even with Nate. The possibility is slim, but still a valid possibility. I decide to head into the woods to see if I can find anything that matches some of these recent evidence pieces I collected.

The silence in the woods is eerie. I pause for a moment staring up in the abyss of tree tops. I have my eyes open but can hardly see. It's still light out and midday beyond these woods. Flashlight in hand waving back and forth aimlessly. I pull my eyes from the tree tops to the ground; I must have walked this spot a thousand times or more in the last few days. We aren't far from the tree line, and the entry into the woods behind the abandoned barn is only a hundred feet or so away. I swear I have looked at this very clump of dirt, this very tree and the same brush marks through the dirt that look like a broom has passed through a dozen times. When the wind whips through here during the storms, it clears all the print anyone has left behind. Who would be able to tell them apart at this point even if there were prints? I can see trees in my sleep, wandering in my dreams in hopes to find this poor girl.

The silence is interrupted briefly by the ring of my cell phone in my pocket. The call we have been waiting for has finally arrived.

The red rag recovered by Nate that Hannah possessed has saliva that matches Rebecca. So, at some point the rag was over Rebecca's mouth, or maybe even in her mouth. There was a very small amount of chemicals left on the rag, which was a very diluted form of chloroform. Would have been strong enough to keep someone quiet for about an hour, but not much longer than that. Not nearly as strong as the chloroform we have found in some cases. Which leads me to believe this was a homemade concoction. Sometimes just because you know the chemical components doesn't mean you can master making something.

There was some blood on the screw, but it was such a small amount, the lab in the city wasn't able to match it to anything. They are sending it to a federal facility. They have better machines than we could ever have. This phone call sucks. All the hope I had that we are looking for Rebecca alive is gone. I think we are definitely looking for a body now.

The rest of the team has been equipped with really expensive metal detectors. Disheartening, the feeling of moving on to look for a body than to be looking for an alive and well young lady. The office sent out for the metal detectors a few days ago, and received them just this morning. Even though this is a very serious matter, the officers are like kids in candy stores ready to play with their new toys. I admire that it has given them a boost of energy, though.

They started at the other side of the woods moving towards where I stand now. With no real clue on where Rebecca may be. We really have to go through the entire acreage to be sure we are doing our jobs correctly.

I find myself dazing. I can't keep focused. I am on my sixth cup of coffee, and it's shortly after noon. My wife would be scolding me if she knew. Thinking about what this family must be going through. If anything ever happened to my children,I couldn't stand to look at myself. Especially being on the force. The phone call has me perplexed; this must have been a thought-out process.

Is a student really capable of premeditated murder?

Could Hannah really be the one responsible for all of this?

Low tones of beeping in the background sweeping their way through the woods towards myself. I am still standing in the same spot. I can't put my finger on it, but something about this tree makes me feel like there is something here. I hope that I am wrong, desperate hope. One of the deputies comes from around the corner and *BEEP BEEP BEEP.*

"Here! Here!"

"Everyone, come this way!Y!" I have my flashlight in the air waving frantically to get everyone's attention.

"Come over here!"

 "Grab the shovels!"

"We found something!"

"Over here!"

Every police officer in the woods comes running in my direction, carrying shovels and sifters to look through the soil. Running as quickly as they can, a herd of elephants running scared. They all stop in front of the spot where the metal detector went off.

"How do you want to do this, Cap?" The officer looks at me out of breath and puzzled. The fact that we may have found something has us all out of sorts. None of the officers want it to be Rebecca. Denial at its best, we want it to be something random and to find Rebecca hiding in the barn somewhere.

"Let's dig away from the metal spot just in case. And carefully, don't just dig right in."

"Eric, take the metal detector and track the metal spots. Let's make sure we don't dig right into the hot spot. She might be down there." I gulp audibly as I finish that sentence. *Please don't let that be the case* is all I keep thinking.

The Deputy sweeps the area about a five-foot by four-foot section. Just enough for a body below. We all start to dig around the spot, and about two feet into the ground, a loud thunk from the shovel hitting something below. Everyone stops. You could hear a pin drop with the silence that has overcome us.

"Okay, okay. We are going to keep going. We can go two feet to get whatever this is visible, but be very delicate."

The officers all take turns digging about two feet worth of dirt off the object. As we start the clear, the object becomes visible, and we all come to the realization at the same time.

This is a box.

Once we clear the heavy soil from on top of the box, we all grab paint brushes to dust the dirt off in order to find the sides.

"Alright guys, everyone put gloves on grab a side and let's get this up." I am trying to stay calm, although I have so much anxiety flowing through me, I can barely hold it together. We pull the top of the box up and off, walking it off to the side. Tears are gushing down my face, and I can't control them any longer. Could be the lack of sleep or the thought that we've found Rebecca, and we have always been looking for a body, not a girl.

No one moves or speaks for what seems like hours, but must only have been a few minutes. The sadness has completely taken over the occupied space around.

Rebecca died inside this box.

From the look of her finger tips, she was alive when she was put into it. We call the paramedics and the coroner, and then we decide to wait to call the parents. They shouldn't see her in this state.

Rebecca's once golden hair is covered in dirt, leaves and moss; she must have been dragged on the ground. She is bloated from being dead for the last few days. Based on her skin color being greenish, she died about twelve to twenty four hours after being put into this box. She must have been in the box since the night she was reported missing. She didn't have a lot of oxygen in there. Foam with some blood has leaked from her mouth and her nose all over her face. Her eyes are still wide open and bloodshot, several broken blood vessels that pooled. There is a glaze over her eyes like the elderly get with cataracts.

Her fingertips are mostly gone. I have the deputy flip the top of the box over, and some of her fingernails are stuck within the wood grain. She was trying to claw her way out the best that she could. I can't even fathom the last things she was thinking of or feeling. The paramedics arrive and declare the death, which is protocol even though we can clearly see. The coroner and the paramedics work on taking Rebecca's body out of the box. When they lift her to the gurney, her whole back is covered in what looks like bruising. The coroner says that is from her blood pooling to her back from lying in the same spot so long post mortem. I follow the paramedics and the coroner to the van to see Rebecca off.

"Wait, Cap!"

I flip my body around 180 so quickly I almost lose my balance. "What is it?"

"There's something in here!" He gets on his hands and knees and reaches down into the box. He pulls out a book and starts to flip through the pages, shuffling them like playing cards.

"It's a journal, but I don't think it's hers." He looks up to me and places the book in my open hand.

"Oh no. We have to bring this to Dr. Psych."

CHAPTER 17 - DR. PSYCH

Present

I have been a practicing psychiatrist for the last fifteen years. I have been seeing Hannah since her parents started the divorce, when her and her mother moved here. It's amazing the things she is capable of. Hannah reads and retains so much information—the intelligence that she has I envy. Her mother was always so fearful for her.

Her father was incredibly intelligent also. Hannah took more qualities from her father than from her mother. Which made the fear grow for her mother. Obviously, Hannah has some of the same issues that her father has as well. Her technical diagnosis is schizophrenia with a touch of dissociative amnesia. Hannah struggles with her thinking, feeling and behavior. She has never had hallucinations, but has often suffered from delusions and very disorganized thinking. Her delusions involve firm beliefs that things are happening or have happened that are simply not true, or in some extreme cases not real. She has only had a few moments where she has lost complete touch of reality, and I am afraid that Rebecca may have been one of those moments. Dissociative amnesia adds to some of her delusions. Best explained as losing all memory in stressful or traumatic experiences. Since we figured out the right dosage on her medicine, she hasn't had any what I call "episodes".

I was very concerned when Hannah told me about Rebecca. She had no recognition of not mentioning her before in my office, and I could see in her face she was completely dumbfounded. That was when I realized her medicine wasn't in check. The way that she explained the relationship between her and Rebecca sounded like this has been going on for some time. For her to only bring her up last week, especially given the circumstances, was out of character. To add to the fact that she was completely taken off guard that Rebecca was missing, and had no recollection of anything past the party.

I fear that as I am putting the pieces together the worst may have happened. The Captain brought me a journal from the unfortunate site they found Rebecca. As I read through the page, my fears became real life circumstance.

Hannah wrote this.

The body was found two days ago now. Hannah has been in the hospital three days following an attack from another student during her police interview. I have read the journal front to back multiple times in the last two days, examining every page and every word, line for line. Hannah was unmedicated for some time, going back a minimum of six months ago. That is a lot of time for a schizophrenic to go unmedicated—her delusions must have been quite strong.

I meet with the Captain in a few minutes, and then with Hannah's mother afterwards, to share the information I have collected. It is probably for the best that they don't actually read any of these passages, but I will explain as much as I can based on what I have found.

I walk into the room, and the Captain is flipping through pages of a suspect report. My guess would be Hannah's. It's small—they must not have done a ton of research on her because they couldn't connect her to the crime. I wonder what they have found since then.

"Captain." I nod my head towards him as I take my seat in his office.

"Doctor." He nods back in reply

"I assume you have done more research on Hannah since we first spoke last week. I would have to also assume you have some questions." I set the journal down in front of me and watch him shudder as it touches his desk.

"Yes, Doctor I have a few questions, but the one that is burning me terribly is why would you let this girl into public school after the history the family has?"

"Well, Captain, people do change. I believe that when medicated, Hannah is a completely normal, functioning adolescent, no more erratic than one who is going through a hormonal change." I answer matter-of-factly, knowing that he is convinced that once someone is crazy in his definition, they are always crazy.

"I accept your response, although I don't agree." He breathes deeply, prepared for the next question that I know is coming and he isn't ready for the answer.

"In your professional opinion, Doctor, do you think Hannah buried Rebecca in the box underground?"

I hold the key to all the answers in this moment for him, and he knows it.

"Yes. I actually know that she did."

"Why? Why would she do that?!" He snaps at me.

"I don't know that you will like this answer, but basically the delusion that Hannah was having ended and met reality. For a schizophrenic who is unmedicated for a long period of time, when reality comes to light and meets the fictional story they have been writing in their head, it's very dangerous. I am going to meet with Hannah's mother, where I am going to explain this whole journal. If you choose to sit in, I am giving you my permission. You may not have an outburst during that session; this is going to be very tough for

Hannah's mother to take in. If you wish, I will also talk to Rebecca's parents afterwards and explain what I can to them as well. Only if you think they are ready to hear it." I feel very confident with my response. I know that this isn't easy for anyone, but I will stand my ground.

"I would like to be there when you talk to her. If I have to, I will excuse myself from the situation. You have to know that I just need to understand what happened. I apologize for my outburst."

Both relieved with this end to the conversation, we part ways and I go back to my office.

Trisha should be here momentarily. I am staring at the pictures of my tubby little tabby Bruno. I have sat so many times with Hannah in this room, talking and watching her body language. How did I let this go on for so long without noticing the behavior? The death of this girl is my fault. If I would have picked up on her not taking her medicine, I could have institutionalized her. Hannah could have mainstreamed after a few weeks of everyday treatment, and we would have been back to normal without a young woman being dead. I am sure that Trisha is thinking all of the same things I am right now. I swing my hand next to my face as if to push the negativity out of my way so I clear my head. Show a brave face while I tell Hannah's mother everything she wrote in this journal, which is pretty hard to read. I hear the squeak of my overly excited-at-all-times receptionist.

Trisha must be here.

The Captain is here as well, waiting in the office. I have to discuss with Trisha if she is comfortable with him sitting in on our meeting. I know that she won't say no, but it's courteous to ask her first.

"Good afternoon, Trisha. How are you holding up?"

"I am doing okay. Hannah is still out, but the doctor said they should be able to wake her up within a few days. I haven't slept or eaten much. The hospital food is terrible, and I can't stand the thought of leaving her there alone for long periods of time."

I don't think I have ever seen her without makeup on. Her hair is tied in a bun on top of her head, and doesn't appear as though she has been home much in the last few days. Her mental health is hanging on by a thread, the sags to her eyes verify her not sleeping much. I truly do feel for her. More than one family is impacted by this tragedy.

"Trisha, I have to make sure you are okay with this before we head into my office. The Captain has asked to sit in on this meeting so he can hear what was written in this journal. Would that be acceptable? It is okay to say no. This is a sensitive subject," I say while trying to gauge her reaction.

"Yes. That's fine." Short response, and a saddened tone.

I open my office door and wave my hand to let her know she may enter and choose wherever she would like to sit. The Captain and Trisha exchange pleasantries, and Trisha takes the seat next to him. I sit down in my chair behind my desk. The journal lying on the desk open in the center, neither of them lean over to read it. I think the information inside makes them uneasy.

"Thank you both for coming, and I want to stress the severity of the situation. What is written in this journal by Hannah is mildly disturbing. I am going to start from the beginning, and if at any time you wish for me to stop, please say so. I am not going to read you the passages. I have decided to summarize for this meeting and will be handing the journal over to the police once we are finished here. It is considered evidence. Do we understand each other before we move forward?"

They both take a deep breath in and reply simultaneously.

"Yes."

"Alright, let's get started. Based on this journal and what Hannah was experiencing, she was unmedicated for at least the last six months. This journal starts at a birthday party for Rebecca based on how Hannah wrote it. She was not an invited guest. She walked around the back of the house and found herself a seat to observe the party. She never wrote about any interactions with anyone else, so my assumption is she didn't talk to anyone there. She may have even been in a place where no one noticed she was there to begin with. This is where her obsession with Rebecca started. Hannah decided that she was going to be on the stage crew for the school play because Rebecca was trying out for the lead role. We all were so happy that she was engaging in school activities that none of us thought twice about *why*. Hannah had an interaction with Rebecca that was genuine and actually very sweet. She helped her find something and her excitement was the sweetest thing I have read from her in a very long time. But here's where Hannah started to take a turn. She writes about these Friday night adventures at the mall, which Trisha, I know that you are aware that she was going— that's not the concerning part. Rebecca had no idea that Hannah was following her on her Friday night shopping trips. They were not meeting each other and being the standard teenage girls at the mall. Hannah followed her to each stop she made and waited for her to move on from afar. She even has a picture from outside of the dress store attached in the journal, where she was watching Rebecca try on her prom dress. Hannah mentions that they sat together and had a pretzel, but based on the scenario, I believe she was sitting a few tables away and watching Rebecca. Rebecca was under the impression she was alone at the mall every Friday for a few months." As I finish this sentence, Trisha is holding her hands to her face and tears are streaming down. I can see the discomfort that this is causing in her and the Captain. Rebecca was none the wiser to Hannah being around her at every turn she took. Unsettling to say the least.

"I can stop if you would like. Unfortunately, it doesn't get better from here." I am trying to give a way out in case they are ready to end the conversation.

Trisha regains her composure and looks at me directly in the eye. "No, I need to know. Please keep going."

"Part of Hannah's disorder is that, to her, this imaginary story of what she has written is completely real. She truly believed that she and Rebecca were friends, and that they were doing all of these things together. Trisha, Hannah was drugging you to go out late at night to the parties. She explains in her journal that she would make ice cream on any of the nights she needed to get out. She put some sleeping meds mixed into some chocolate curls that she topped your ice cream with. She learned after the first party where you caught her that she needed to change her tactic. Let's go to the night of the party where Rebecca went missing." I pause and look at the Captain. He crosses his hands over his lap, fingers intertwined. This is the part he is really interested in. Trisha is sitting at the edge of her seat holding her breath and grasping her chest.

"The night of the party, Hannah started by having ice cream with you, Trisha. She arrived at the party and was met by what I thought was another student, but I have come to believe is just a person she was imagining. She mentioned him in one of the conversations last week—Raymond. He seems to come about when she needs him the most, and I don't believe that he is a real person. It seems as though he is a figment of her imagination created by her subconscious. While Hannah was drinking and participating in some conversation with Raymond, Rebecca went into the woods. Rebecca was gone for a period of time that didn't seem acceptable to Hannah, so her reaction was to go find her. When Hannah arrived into the woods, she startled Rebecca, and this was where reality met the fiction.

Rebecca turned around and confronted Hannah about what she was doing and why she was there. Hannah didn't like that Rebecca wasn't acting like they had been friends for the last few months and had spent so much time together. To Hannah, it was a betrayal. To Rebecca it was confusion, none of what Hannah thought was happening had actually happened. Part of the delusion she had created. This very real moment for Hannah sent her spiraling. She learned how to make a form of chloroform in chemistry. Based on what follows, subconsciously she had a plan to take Rebecca at some point if it wasn't this night. She had all the material needed in her bag with her, including a red rag she had taken from class. Hannah quickly poured the chloroform onto the rag and shoved it into Rebecca's face. While Rebecca was on the ground, Hannah snuck into the barn and grabbed the materials that she needed to build the box and dig a hole in the ground deep enough that no one would see that Rebecca was buried there. Rebecca was too heavy for Hannah to lift, so she had to drag her into the box. After she sealed the box with a lid and started to put the dirt over, Rebecca woke up. She was screaming at her. Hannah continued."

"I have to go. I can't do this. Thank you, Dr. Psych," the Captain interrupts, standing and advancing to the door.

"That's okay, Captain. I know this isn't easy. Please let me know what you need from me. I will continue if you wish, Trisha."

The Captain closes the door from behind him, leaving Trisha and I alone.

"I have a question. How do you know what happened that night? Are you speculating?"

"No. Unfortunately, Hannah wrote it all down. She was still sitting at the sight, listening to Rebecca scream for her, while she wrote down everything that had just happened."

"Oh my god, Hannah, how could this go so wrong?" Trisha is beside herself.

"There is a little more if you would like me to continue, or we can stop for now. I wrote some notes so that we didn't have to do this in one sitting. I know this is overwhelming to hear from your daughter."

She chokes back her tears. "No, I am okay. Go on."

"Hannah realized that something wasn't right. She expressed the dream she had of being buried alive. She was living through Rebecca, and imagining what it must have been like for her. I find myself wondering now if she thought all of it was a dream, or if there is zero memory from this night at all. She may recall some bits and pieces as she is medicated and monitored—only time will tell on that. When she came home that night, she took her medicine, and the next morning when she woke up, she had no recollection of the events. She wrote that everything in her mind was a fog, and she uses the reference to puzzle pieces not fitting together often. Hannah had another episode where Raymond came into play and asked her to join him in the search for Rebecca. That night, she found Rebecca's necklace in the woods, and although it didn't spark any memory for her, she decided to wear it after that point. I noticed it here in my office, and Nate, Rebecca's boyfriend noticed it during the interview. Which, my guess would be, was what set him off. Hannah witnessed Rebecca receiving the necklace for her birthday. It was special. She wore it everyday after her birthday. Hannah put it on because it gave her a reconnection to Rebecca, as if Rebecca gave it to her for safekeeping in the event of her going missing. I know that doesn't make much sense to you, but to Hannah, it was the only way to keep the memory of Rebecca and their imaginary friendship alive." I pause to look up at Hannah's mother. What a heart-breaking experience this must be to know that your daughter could commit such a horrible act and have no recollection of the event at all.

"Trisha, I think it best that we have a few sessions ourselves in the weeks to come so I can help you understand what is going to happen with Hannah. She is going to be placed in a facility similar to your ex-husband, and as time grows, she will gain new privileges and be moved to more open facilities. Hannah has committed murder, and she will unfortunately stand trial, but mentally ill is the standpoint I will help prove in court. I know this is so much to take in. When Hannah wakes, I would like to visit with her if you allow."

"Yes, of course, Dr. Psych. I welcome you—you have been so helpful over the years. I just can't put together in my mind how things could have been so wrong. I have so many questions for her, and it sounds like she will never really have the answers to give me from this amnesia she experiences. I lost my husband, and now my daughter to things out of my control."

I grab the tissue box and join her on the opposite side of my desk. Rubbing her back and reassuring her there was nothing she could have done to change what happened. There was no way for us to know what was happening inside Hannah's head without her revealing it. Most of what happened will remain a mystery to us all, including Hannah.

What Hannah calls a misplaced memory will never quite fit back into the puzzle the way that it should.

ABOUT THE AUTHOR

"Misplaced Memory" is my debut novel. Let me introduce myself. I am the proud mom of one spontaneous little boy Owen and a bonus mom of three. Our oldest son Anthony, middle son Ricky and daughter Natalie. What a rewarding experience to be a part of their lives the last 11 years.

My husband and I met by chance but who knew it would lead to all this. We own a salvage yard in Brockport, NY selling used auto parts, a repair shop in Clarendon NY, we are auto dealers and we have so many more things we want to start up.

I have always been a creative person not an artist by any means but I love to create new things. I make t-shirts for our shops and stickers and I create fun things for my son's spirit weeks at school. I have actually started to think of taking that to the next level for myself as well. I do mugs and dip into sublimation a tad and I enjoy doing diamond art to keep myself moving. Really it's fun for me. Most people I talk to ask where the time comes from and sometimes I don't even know I am a busy person but finding time to enjoy some of the things I want is important to me.

I was lying in bed one night and came up with this story idea in my head. I messaged my cousin and said, I'm crazy to think I could do this too. She replied absolutely not, you better write it. It hasn't been very long and once I got to typing the words just flowed through my fingers. Note: I did not live this and it is not a personal story. My stories are just that.

I am so grateful for those of you who have been incredibly supportive already and I hope you enjoy this journey with me!

ACKNOWLEDGEMENTS

I cannot express enough in words how thankful I am to my cousin Sarah Asermily for pushing me in the direction to start writing. Not only has she helped me with the entire process from start to finish but she has been the number one person to cheer me on since the start. I offer my sincere appreciation to her and everything she has done to guide my way.

My completion of my debut novel could not have been accomplished without the support and love of my husband. To my husband Richard- Thank you for always telling me to pick up my work and keep moving. Thank you for listening to me read chapter after chapter to you when we should have been sleeping. The countless amount of times you have listened to me talk about my novel and run ideas past you. Richard, you have truly been on this adventure alongside me.

Finally to my friends and family who have been so interested in my novel to support, share and express excitement. I could not have made it this far without you!

Printed in the USA
CPSIA information can be obtained
at www.ICGtesting.com
CBHW031050030824
12553CB00041BA/889